HAUNT

Vicky,
you're the
best

A BAYONET SCARS NOVEL

HAUNT

Love is never more beautiful than when it consumes you.

JC EMERY

HAUNT (BAYONET SCARS, NO. 6)

ISBN-13: 9781536875904
ISBN-10: 1536875902

Cover Design by Brenda Gonet at Star Bound Books
Formatting by
Editing by Michele Milburn

MATURE CONTENT WARNING
The Bayonet Scars novels are a dark and gritty romance series which features graphic sexual content, violence, and foul language that is intended for a mature audience. Each novel features a different couple, though it's not recommended that they be read out of order due to the series story arc.

SERIES & TITLES BY JC EMERY

Bayonet Scars

Ride (No. 1)

Thrash (No. 2)

Rev (No. 3)

Crush (No. 4)

Vow (No. 4.5)

Burn (No. 5)

Crave (No. 5.5)

Haunt (No. 6)

Cease (No. 7)

For Mandie,

I couldn't do this without you.

PROLOGUE

Amber

June 2001

I reach out from the warm cocoon I've created for myself in our bed. My hand slides across the cold sheets as if I'm going to find him there. I know he's left me again. I felt him get out of our bed the moment my breathing evened out and he thought I was asleep. Just like every other night since he accused me of being pregnant.

In all fairness, I am. But still. We weren't trying, but we weren't being very careful either, so in a way, we should have expected that second blue line to show up.

We're happy about it.

Well, *I* am.

His daddy used to be.

Now I'm not so sure.

During the day, Wyatt is devoted and loving but still a badass. He's the man I fell in love with back when he was still a boy. But as the day wears on, he becomes less and less of the man I know and more of a cold-blooded soldier for the club. I hate it. I used to party with him, but now he has me tucked safely into bed every night while he does things he thinks I don't know about.

And I'm sick of it. Sick of everything. And he's too stupid and self-absorbed to see what's really happening here.

It's not the baby that makes me sick to my stomach every morning. It's the overwhelming smell of perfume and sex that radiates off of him as he crawls into our bed. He doesn't even shower before wrapping me in his arms and rubbing my belly.

"Don't give me any trouble tonight, you got that?" I say to my rounded stomach. Our baby is a little hellion. He acts up at all hours, but especially at night. He kicks at my ribs and pushes on my bladder, and the only thing that calms him down is if I give him some attention. All I have to do is be busy doing something else and he starts acting like I don't talk to him all freaking day and we don't spend every single second together. Lord help me if this is any indication of what's to come once he's born. I might have to follow in my own mother's footsteps and add a little whiskey to his bottles.

Baby Z—that's what Wyatt likes to call him—adjusts his position and sits his little baby ass right on top of my bladder. While he makes himself more comfortable, he makes me uncomfortable. Not that he cares. As my dad keeps reminding me, it's not about me anymore, and it'll never be about me again. My dad's words play in my head on repeat as I waddle to the bathroom to get ready.

"It's not about you anymore, kid."

I try to fight off the sinking depression that settles in as I flush the toilet and wash my hands. The girl I see in the mirror is unrecognizable. She's not the fun, crazy girl I was seven months ago. She's not full of life and so in love that it borders on obsession.

No, that girl's gone.

That girl was sixteen.

The girl I see in the mirror is seventeen. She's already somebody's old lady. She's about to be a mother. And she has no clue what she's doing anymore.

"Let's see what your daddy's up to." My eyes are fixed on my little boy—well, of his current accommodations—who is kicking at my ribcage. I give him a poke and try to explain the situation so he'll settle down. "I can't bust balls if you keep kicking me this hard. Quit knocking me off my game."

A woman walks by my SUV and turns her nose up in my direction. My window is down, so I know she heard me. People do this—especially lost girls. They either judge me for talking to my kid, or they judge me for being knocked up with my kid—all the time. I wiggle out of the SUV and straighten my back as I waddle toward the front door of the clubhouse. She's walking ahead of me, purposefully slow, and when she gets to the door, she holds it open for me.

"Trying to figure out who the dad is?" she asks in a snide voice.

I roll my eyes and pull my long, reddish brown hair over my shoulder so she can see exactly who she's talking to as I walk by. I spent twenty minutes hunting for this top specifically. It's an old Forsaken tee that's all cut up and tied back together on the sides and over the shoulders to give it a sexy vibe with the back shredded down to my bra strap. It's one of the few sexy things that fits me these days, and it perfectly displays the large tattoo of my man's name on my back.

Turning around and giving her a cocky smirk, I say, "Bitch, please."

The clubhouse is dark inside, but not nearly as dark as the one in Detroit. I don't know if I like it or not. Everything here is so different than it is back home.

This is home now, I remind myself.

Mom died and Dad lost his shit, gave up the gavel in Detroit in favor of leading the California Nomads, and moved me and Michele out here—to Fort Bragg. Just like he promised, Wyatt followed, and just like my dad promised, the Fort Bragg Forsaken have accepted me as one of their own. It wasn't a given that Fort Bragg would recognize me as Wyatt's old lady since Detroit was where I was voted in, but they have. Not that it means much right now, because Wyatt still wears his Detroit patch. He's hesitant to talk to Jim about being patched in to Fort Bragg—mostly because it means leaving Rig, his mentor, but also because his mom is still in Michigan—but I have faith that the longer he continues to work with the brothers out here, the more comfortable he'll feel making this change permanent.

"Shouldn't you be at home?" my sister asks from behind me. She's one to talk. The little twerp is barely sixteen. I'd know her voice anywhere, but especially here. It's one of the few things that remind me of a time when our mom was alive and everything was normal.

Mom died just over a year ago, but it feels like it's been eons since she took her final breath.

"You're kidding me, right?" I turn around, waiting to roll my eyes until she has the benefit of seeing my displeasure for herself, and place a hand on my belly. "Does Dad even know you're here?"

"I doubt he even knows where *he* is," she says and rolls her eyes. I don't argue because she has a point. Since Mom died, our dad's been semipermanently checked out, and ever since he dumped us in Fort Bragg, he's been MIA except for the few times he's popped into town to make sure we're still alive. "Besides, it's not like anything's happening tonight anyway."

"Just don't get anybody arrested," I say and give her the best of my serious expressions. She likes to flirt with the brothers and prospects, but she's way underage, and I don't want to see anyone doing time for tapping her—even if she's asking for it. Mom was great at dirty looks. Michele never acted like this when Mom was still alive. Our mom never failed to convey her displeasure with a single look. She seriously gave the best hairy eyeball I've ever seen—and I've seen a lot of hairy eyeballs. I don't do them nearly as well as she did, judging by the flippant expression on my little sister's face. She's such a little bitch sometimes.

"Yeah, yeah," she says and walks off toward the front door. I have to give up trying to play mom with that one. Pretty soon I'm going to have my hands full with my own kid, and Michele is going to be left to her own devices.

God help her.

I leave all thoughts of my sister behind as I make my way down the hall to the pleasure palace. We don't talk about it, but I know damn well that Wyatt hangs out in here more than he should. And considering his old lady is knocked up and waddling, he shouldn't be hanging out in here at all. But the brothers play by their own rules, and they don't give a damn what I think. The chaos of the clubhouse dies down the farther I get down the hall. Men walk by me, some in cuts and some not. They don't pay me any mind, and I like it that way. I'm not supposed to be here, and anybody who knows me well enough knows that. It's not like Rage gives a shit what I do, but Wyatt told me to stay home in front of everyone, and that means I'm to stay home. Your old man's word is law when it comes to the club, and it doesn't matter that it's total bullshit. It only matters that that's what he wants, and so I'm to stay home.

But it doesn't feel like home, and I don't like it there. I don't like my bed because it smells like other women no matter how many times I change the sheets. It's not the kitchen my mom used to make pancakes in. It's not the bathroom I used to fight with Michele over. As much as I want to make this place work for me—for our little family—it just doesn't feel like home yet.

Knowing my man is here with other women and high off his ass makes staying home feel like a prison sentence. And my only crime was falling in love with a liar.

The double doors of the pleasure palace open, and a group of people stumble out. I move out of their way and steel myself for making it through those doors but pause when I see a familiar face. Rig, Detroit's new president and my dad's former VP, stands in the doorway with his eyes fixed on me. Great.

"Go home, babe," he says with a shake of his head.

"That an order?"

He shrugs his shoulders and looks around, then says, "No, but it should be. Your old man's gonna be pissed."

"I know," I say. Rig's always been good to me. He doesn't treat me like a kid like a lot of my dad's brothers do. "I can't take it anymore. I know the code, Rig, but he doesn't even try to hide what he's doing."

"You remember what we talked about when you were voted in?"

I try to keep a stiff upper lip and not show my hurt at the memory.

"This is the life. Brothers do what they're gonna do, and old ladies turn the other cheek."

"Yeah," he says and waves me over. He opens his arms and wraps me in an awkward hug. My belly gets in the way of everything these days. I've known Rig for years now. This isn't the first hug he's ever given me, but it is the first one since I became an old lady. I'm not to be touched and we both know this. The only man who's allowed to touch me, unless it's for my safety, is my old man. Nobody would give a shit if my dad hugged me, but a patched brother putting his hands on another brother's old lady is a no-no. The only thing worse would be if a stranger did it, but this is Rig—it's not like that between us.

"Those rules are bullshit. We tell our women to turn the other cheek, but you bitches never listen. I ain't gonna rat you out, but I didn't see you either," he says.

I pull back from our hug, but he holds me tight to his body. His hands start to move and rub my back in a slow, circular motion. This doesn't feel okay anymore. I feel his head dip and his nose brush against the top of my head as he sucks a deep breath in. I don't want him touching me or breathing me in or anything. Rig's my old man's president, so I can't just push him away. I mean, I probably could, but the prospect scares me for some reason. I can't put my finger on it, but there's something in the way Rig's holding me that sets off my warning bells.

"Man, found your girl wandering around alone," Rig says as he clears his throat. My hands fall to my sides immediately. He releases me, and I step back and swing around as quickly as I can with my burgeoning belly.

Wyatt stands halfway down the hall with his arms folded over his chest. His glare is icy, and even from here I can see how tense he is. My man is hot as hell. He's always been hot, but the more he works out and the bigger his muscles get, the sexier he is to me. His short dark-brown hair is mussed, his broad shoulders heave, and his incredible jaw is locked in place. My hormones are so out of control that I actually have to remind myself that I'm mad at him.

"Good thing you found her, boss." Wyatt is responding to Rig, but he's looking at me. His words are clipped. There's so much anger emanating from him that it's starting to freak me out.

I'm angry.

He's cheating on me.

No. He's cheating on us.

My hand finds its way to my belly in a protective manner. Wyatt won't hit me, but this situation has my hair standing on end. I don't like my baby being in the middle of this, but since he goes where I go, I don't have a choice.

"If you're busy, I can take her home," Rig says. Wyatt's body jerks at his president's words, and he storms down the hall toward us. I make the mistake of taking a step backward—a move my man doesn't miss—giving him the wrong impression. In a second, he's on me, his hand hooked around the back of my neck, and pulls me into his side. It's not loving like I want him to be. He radiates anger and hate in a way I've never felt from him before. We've had our fights, and they get heated, but this is different.

"You wear that patch, so I'll give you the respect it calls for," Wyatt says as he shoves a finger at Rig's president patch. "But you've been put on notice. This woman belongs to me. The next time you touch her, I'll rip your fucking arm off and fuck your mother with it."

Rig smirks and places his hands on his hips like he's enjoying this. When he finally talks, I'm wishing he'd just kept his mouth shut. "Your woman came to me, son. She's lonely and looking for something you're obviously not giving her. You want to fuck someone, maybe you should try fucking your girl so she's not up on my dick."

With the flip of his wrist, Wyatt sends me for the wall behind me. My shoulders and head hit the exposed brick at the same time. I lose my vision for just a moment, but it's long enough for Wyatt to jump Rig and the two men to have each other locked in death grips with their noses shoved together.

"Wyatt, baby, he's lying," I say. My head throbs and my shoulders ache, but I have to tell Wyatt the truth. I don't know what game Rig's playing at, but he's full of shit. I'm not up on his dick, nor have I ever been. "Calm down. Don't do this."

If someone else was here, Wyatt would probably be in the clear because Rig fucking taunted him. But we're alone, and it's the president's word versus a non-office-holding brother and his old lady, and our relationship isn't exactly picture-perfect right now. Wyatt won't lose his patch over this, but it won't end well for him either.

"Tell me you love me, baby," Wyatt says on a plea. He's gasping for air and still locked in Rig's death grip, but I have all his attention.

"Every ounce and every breath," I say. He said those words to me once—that every ounce of him and every breath he takes is for me and me alone. That he'd rather die than be away from me.

Wyatt grunts and then, in a massive show of his strength, shoves Rig off of him. He pulls back enough to eye up the man he considers his mentor. And then he snaps. Wyatt wails on Rig with a show of hatred he's never exhibited before. It's intense, the way he slams his fist into the older man's face and ribs with absolutely no remorse or doubt. Rig fights back, and even gets in a few good hits, but for the most part he's out-matched. They're nearly equal in height, but Wyatt puts so much time into lifting that even with the heavy drinking and drugs he's still a fucking killing machine—and he's just unleashed all his rage on his president.

When Rig is good and bloody and cowering on the floor, Wyatt finally lets up. He bends down and holds Rig by his hair and hisses words of disgust into the man's face. "You're not my president, and you're not my fucking brother."

I stand motionless as I watch Wyatt kick Rig one more time and then disappear through the doors of the pleasure palace. I follow without even thinking, so desperate to have some resolution to this thing between us. I didn't do anything wrong—not really, anyway—and I need him to do something to give me faith that he's still the same man I fell in love with. Anything would do at this point.

But he doesn't do anything to reassure me that he loves me and he's committed to our son. He just strides through the pleasure palace, ignoring every woman who eyes his massive frame, and heads for one of the couches in a far corner of the room. I watch as the man I love plops down on the sofa, shoving a man without a cut out of the way, and snaps his fingers at the woman holding the small mirror flat in her hands. She lifts the mirror up for him and hands him a short, cut-up straw. He leans in, puts the straw in his nose, and sucks up one line after another. I hate that he does this. He didn't used to. The coke is a fairly new thing for him. Everything's changed since he patched in. Slowly but surely he's become someone I barely recognize. Back when he was a hang-around, and even when he was a prospect, he was rarely high or drunk.

He only indulged a little, and even then I could still talk to him. But now, when he's like this, it's impossible. I can't help but try anyway.

"Baby, talk to me." My voice sounds foreign to my own ears. I'm desperate and needy. I hate those girls, but with Wyatt, that's who I become.

"How long?"

"What?" I have no idea what he's even talking about now. It's all half sentences and coded language when he's in a bad mood.

"How long have you been letting him fuck you?"

"Never. I told you he's full of shit. Every night I'm at home in our bed waiting for you."

"You let him touch you," he says with an icy coldness to his voice that makes me uneasy.

"It was a hug and I'm sorry." My voice is small and tears pool in my eyes. I've never been much of a crier, but the last trimester is really fucking with me.

Wyatt stands from the couch, wipes his nose, and stalks over to me. He grabs me behind my neck again and pulls me in close to him so our faces are as close as they can get with our son between us.

"Fuck, you're beautiful," he says. His other hand palms my belly and then slides around to my ass. His hand squeezes at my sensitive flesh in ways that both pinch and burn. "Every ounce and every breath."

"Take me to a room," I say as seductively as I can. If I can distract him with sex, then maybe this will blow over a little quicker.

"Tell me he forced you," he whispers.

I still, wanting to respond but not knowing how. I've spent my entire life around badass bikers, and there's been no shortage of badass bikers who get fucked up and have bad temper tantrums to go with it. All six foot six of Wyatt hovers over me, pressed into me, touching me. I have to find a way to diffuse the situation and quick.

"Tell me, woman." Wyatt's words come out as a bark. I remind myself that this is what the coke does to him. One moment he's gentle and sweet, and the next his eyes are a million miles away and he looks like he's on a super-secret recon mission or something.

"Babe, nothing happened," I say as calmly as I can. I'm not going to lie to appease him—especially not *this* lie. Forcing yourself on another brother's old lady is suicide. If I say what Wyatt wants me to say, it's an automatic death sentence for Rig. I can't and won't do that to someone—regardless of how displeased I may be with them at the moment.

"You lie," Wyatt says. Again, his voice takes on a low whisper that couldn't sound more deadly if he tried. "I see the way he looks at you."

"Seriously?" I snap and try to push him off me. It does no good but to irritate me. Wyatt's pulled this bullshit before, but he's usually over it once the high wears off. "Clear head, baby. I need you to have a clear head."

"Oh, my head's clear, bitch." The words fly out of his mouth like razorblades.

I flinch.

The boy I fell in love with would back off when he saw he was hurting me. But this is the man he's become, and he's not nearly as kind or gentle. No, the man before me sees weakness and he exploits it. It doesn't matter that he promised to love me and to protect me. It doesn't matter that when we conceived our son that it was in the bed we share, and that he told me I'm the most beautiful thing he's ever been able to touch. And it doesn't matter that, like the stupid kid I was, I believed him.

"You've been fucking around behind my back."

I want to tell him he's crazy and that I'd never betray him, but I can't get the words to form in my mouth. It wouldn't matter anyway.

None of it matters because he's a predator and I'm his prey. This is what we've become. Veritable strangers, ready to claw at each other every chance we get. He's always bitching that I'm not the same person I used to be—that I used to be fun and I used to actually like him. Nothing he says is untrue, and so I can't even deny it.

And I can't do it again.

I can't fight about the drugs or the whores or money. Because babies cost money and they need things that I can't afford on my own, but I know damn well that Wyatt can. I can't fight for his affection or attention anymore. This has got to end. My parents were seriously fucked in a bunch of different ways, but even they fought less than we do. If it's like this now, then what is it going to be like when my baby is here?

He places his hands on my ass cheeks and squeezes before sliding them up to my lower back and around to the sides of my belly. I take a deep breath and relax into his touch—but just a little—because he's always calmer after he reminds himself of the power of our love. This baby that kicks at my ribs and pushes on my bladder only exists because we dared fall in love despite everything. Baby Z is made up of the absolute best of who Wyatt and I are, and nothing and no one can ever change that.

"This baby is a fucking lifesaver," he says quietly. His eyes are fixed on our baby. His hands roam from the sides of my stomach up to the top and then down to the bottom. He traces the stretch marks beneath my shirt with his index finger. He can't see them from here, but he's done this so many times, he just knows where they are. Deep inside, behind the confusion and the anger that overtakes him when he gets high, he knows me. He knows me well enough to know the lines on my stomach like they've always been there, even though they're fairly new.

"Yeah, he is." He's calmer now, and we're finally moving past this. I lean up and brush the back of my hand over his cheek. I love this man. Sometimes I just have to remind myself of that.

"Otherwise," Wyatt says slowly and pauses, his voice dropping so low I barely even hear him, "I'd kill you for betraying me."

It takes me a minute to realize what he's said, but by then it's too late. His hands travel up my belly and over my breasts to my neck where he squeezes at my tender flesh. It only hurts a little. Not as much as I thought it would, but enough for me to come to terms with what's happening here. Enough to know that this is it. I can't stay here no matter how much I love him. I can't let this be my baby's future.

"He's not mine," he says. "I still love him too much to hurt you, so I'm going to let you leave."

I stand there motionless and watch as Wyatt releases me and steps back. His eyes are dead and his shoulders are slumped. He's a million miles away.

"Baby, he's yours. I never fucking cheated." It's a plea. A pathetic, desperate, sad-as-fuck appeal to a man I barely know anymore but love anyway.

"Tell me the truth."

Something snaps in me, and I make a choice I can't take back.

And I lie.

"He's not yours." The words come out so slowly and broken that I barely recognize my own voice. It's ridiculous. They're just words, but they mean so much. I don't let myself feel the weight of them, nor do I let myself look Wyatt in the eye. I just stand there and lie like it's the easiest thing to do in the world. It's easier than breathing. It's easier than thinking. I don't like liars, but in this moment I've become one of them. And I don't let myself feel it, because I think if I do, my knees will buckle and I won't be able to leave. And I *really* need to leave now.

"I'm going to get my dick wet. When I'm done, you better be fucking gone."

He turns and leaves.

And then so do I.

I think I've waited long enough to avoid seeing him when I waddle out, but I haven't. To the left of the front door, leaning against the wall with his hands laced behind his head, is Wyatt. He's staring into the hall absently. It's obvious because when he sees me, his eyes flicker to life and his shoulders straighten. I don't have a choice but to pass him on my way out. I make my way slowly down the hall, desperately wanting to move my eyes from his but unable to. A loud man stumbles down the hall and bumps into me. I'm pushed into the wall. I right myself quickly and keep going. I have to swallow the lump in my throat and force one foot in front of the other. And still, my eyes don't leave his.

It isn't until I'm just a few feet away that we break eye contact. He looks down and smirks at his feet. My eyes follow his to find the same woman who made the snotty comment to me on my way in on her knees. She's unbuckling Wyatt's belt and staring up at him like he's a god or something. It's the same look I used to give him. My steps falter. I'm just a few feet from the door, but I can't make myself move. After his belt, she goes for his zipper. She reaches into his boxers, but he—with his eyes still on her—shakes his head and says, "Down."

Wyatt's dick—*my* dick—springs free as she pulls his boxers down. I don't see what her tongue is doing. I don't see anything except for the tattoo above his dick that says my name—a declaration of a forever that's never going to happen.

Because this is the end of us.

CHAPTER ONE

August 2015

8 months to Mancuso's downfall

My stomach rolls as I sit in the passenger seat of my own freaking vehicle. My ass hurts from the long-ass drive out here from Detroit, but it's the handcuffs that link my right wrist to the door handle that bug me the most. I've pulled at them, tried to pick the lock with a bobby pin, and jiggled the fucking things since Diesel slapped 'em on me. Not that I thought my attempts would do any good. They're the same cuffs the cops use, not the soft type you use for sex. Not that I know much of anything about sex these days.

"Is this really necessary?"

Diesel doesn't even look my way before he says, "Yes." I huff, but his jaw ticks and he opens his mouth to speak before I can. "Your boy safe?"

"Yes."

My kids are with my dad and Elle at his house a few miles outside of Fort Bragg. The only reason he's even home is because I told him we were coming in and needed a place to crash. God only knows where he was when we talked. I'm not even sure why the man keeps that house since he's never there.

"Then yeah," Diesel says.

"Something you need to learn—my word is my law. I mean what I say and I say what I mean. I told you I'd face Wyatt, so I am. The cuffs aren't necessary."

He's quiet for a long time, ignoring me like he didn't even hear me. He pulls us onto Main Street, and we drive for a few blocks before things become more familiar. This place was my home once. I knew it well. Detroit doesn't feel much like home anymore—hasn't for a damn long time—but this doesn't feel like home either. The only place I really feel at home is with my kids.

In the distance, I see the Forsaken Custom Cycle sign. It's old and faded and doesn't do much to advertise for the business. Not that the guys do much with the business aside from their own repairs and the occasional upgrade for a local. I steel myself for the sinking feeling in my gut, but it never comes. Instead, a sort of dead weight settles in my belly, telling me that this is much worse than I think it is. I made my choices, and now I have to live with them.

Fuck.

"Looks like you're gonna puke." His voice is void of any judgment, but he's going somewhere with this, I can tell.

We pull into the parking lot of the shop and I'm faced with the closed gates to the clubhouse. I can't see anything beyond the gates because of the black slats in the chain link that keep prying eyes from club business.

I don't realize I have a death grip on the door handle until the sweat from my hand becomes uncomfortable. I left Wyatt because he made me. It wasn't my choice. I didn't want to leave him. I never would have if he'd given me any choice. But I was seven months pregnant and he'd slammed my head into a brick wall. He'd threatened to kill me and then forced me to watch him get his dick sucked on my way out.

Diesel honks the horn, and I have to close my eyes to block out the view of the clubhouse as the gates open. I can't do this. I can't. I fucking can't. My lungs strain for air that isn't coming. I can't do this. Fuck. Every muscle in my body is tight, and I swear to Christ I think I might swallow my goddamn tongue. I double over and use my free arm to cover my head, like if I can hide in this seat, then I won't have to face Wyatt for what I've done. Tears well in my eyes, but I force them back before they can spill down my face. I may be freaking out, but I refuse to cry. I'm an adult, and I made my choices. I have to deal with them.

Diesel puts the SUV in park, cuts the engine, and waits. He doesn't comfort me in any way. He just lets me freak the fuck out and is damn patient while I do it.

I don't know how long it takes me to calm down. I just know that eventually my breathing stabilizes and I figure out how to stop my heart from beating itself right out of my chest. When I sit up and take a deep breath and calmly look over at Diesel, I find he's staring at me with what might be sympathy in his eyes. Or maybe it's boredom.

"Thus the handcuffs," he says as a way of defense. I don't admit that he was probably right to cuff me. "Got mad respect for you, babe. You earned your title as my VP's old lady, you're raising two kids on your own, and my woman loves you, so that means I got love for you. Your title means your life is more important to me than mine is, but get this—regardless of how shit went down, you got my VP's kids, and I put my ass on the line to help save one of them. Those cuffs ain't about disrespect for you. They're about respect for your old man and my brother. Something you need to learn about me is that I'm a family man, and Forsaken is my family. So yes, the cuffs are necessary."

My lips turn up in the corners even though I try to hide my smile. Diesel just shakes his head, gets out of the car, and walks around to my side and uncuffs me only to slap the other end on himself.

"Got Church and I'm already late, so you're going to keep your ass in your old man's room."

"I could just tag along, ya know," I say. Like that would ever happen.

"Crazy bitch," he mutters and drags me toward the clubhouse. There are two other vehicles in the lot and a line of bikes along the side of the building near the entrance. I avoid checking them out, preferring instead to avoid the mental guessing game of figuring out which one belongs to Wyatt. We walk in, but I keep my eyes on the floor the entire time. It's bad enough that I'm here, doing what I'm doing, but it's even worse that I'm handcuffed to a brother in the process. If I weren't so fucked up, I might be able to feel embarrassed about the situation I've found myself in.

Every step is so familiar, like deja vu or something. It's not because the familiarity comes from the last time I was here. I showed up that night fourteen years ago to show my man I was still his woman, even if I was a woman with a waddle. I left that night totally devastated. Wyatt wasn't mine. It was the worst night of my life. Every day after was better than that day. I didn't have my man but I had my baby, and then when I actually *had* my baby, he was perfect and gorgeous. Even if I was the only thing he had in this world, I vowed to be enough for him. The second worst night of my life was realizing that I'd failed. I'm not enough on my own. Zander needs his dad even if his dad is a fucking asshole. The kid is half a foot taller than me now. He's losing his boyish frame and is starting to grow muscles—all over but in his arms especially. I don't think I realized how strong he'd gotten until we got into a fight about his disappearing this past summer and he pushed me out of his way. It took me back to the way Wyatt used to manhandle me, and I flipped out on him. It didn't do any good. I'm not intimidating enough, I guess, and that's the moment I gave up trying to tell myself that I could do this alone.

I just didn't know how *not* to do this alone.

Not just for Zander, but for Piper as well. She's still so young, and she doesn't know any better, but she needs her a daddy. She needs a man who's going to tell her she's the most beautiful girl in the world. She needs him to make her believe that she's worthy and strong and important just for being who she is. Because one day a man is going to try to treat her like crap, and she needs to know that's bullshit and she's worth more. I can tell her all of that, but she won't absorb it the same way coming from me as she will from her father.

Fuck.

Diesel leads me into what I guess is Wyatt's room. I've never been in here—or more accurately, if I've been in here I don't remember. The last time I was here, Wyatt was just visiting from the Detroit charter and we'd occasionally steal away in a room to make love, but he didn't have his own room. The space is totally impersonal. The outside wall is made up of exposed brick and the other three are painted a flat gray. There are scratches and a few stains on the paint. The space is pretty empty with an old wooden dresser, a metal folding chair, and a large bed on a black metal frame. I pause in the doorway for a minute while I eye the bed frame only to realize I've seen it before.

"He still has it."

"Has what?" Diesel's question surprises me. I didn't realize I'd spoken my thought until now.

"Zander was conceived on this bed frame." When I notice my hand on my belly, I pull it away. This was our bed at one time. This was the bed we shared in our home. This was the bed we made love in. This was the bed where my old man used to hold me, tell me that I'm his reason for breathing, and promise himself to me. A golf-ball-size lump forms in my throat, and no matter how many times I try to swallow it, I can't. Diesel uncuffs himself from me and pulls me to the bed where he forces me to sit. He loops the cuffs around a metal bar only to secure my other hand as well so I have no hope of escaping. He leaves me here, on this bed, and shuts the door behind him.

Our old mattress had a pushy spring right in the middle, about two feet from the head in the center. I keep my eyes closed as I search for it. If Wyatt still has the frame, then maybe he has the mattress, too.

My butt wiggles over a spring that uncomfortably stabs the base of my spine. It's like being taken back to high school, even though by then I'd already dropped out. This is our mattress.

And it's in his room.

At the clubhouse.

My throat constricts in response, and I have to look away from the bed just to take a much-needed breath. Too much history assaults me all at once. I think I was in denial until now. I thought about this a lot—coming back here—but never really considered how it'd feel. I figured if I showed my face in this clubhouse, we'd fuck and fight and fuck some more, just like we do every time he comes to Detroit. He'd be fucked up on whatever he was dabbling in at the time, and he'd tell me everything I wanted to hear, and then he'd just disappear on me. Like every other fucking time I've seen him since we stopped being us. Except this time, I'd tell Jim about Zander and Piper and force their hands at sobering him up long enough to fucking remember he's a father. And the kids would visit him. And my life would stay the same except I'd get a break every now and then. If I imagined how shitty the reality would feel, I'd never have let myself consider forcing him to have a part in his kids' lives. Not that I chose this.

My eyes fall on some weird carving pattern on the back of the door. It looks like a tally, and there must be a couple hundred little marks, if not more. Women. I bet he's tallied the number of women he's fucked in my goddamn bed. All the sorrow and guilt and frustration hardens into an icy cold rage.

I don't see anything else anymore.

I don't feel anything else anymore.

I just *hate.*

This room is way too dark. Save for the occasional set of headlights that shine into the short overhead window, everything is completely shrouded in darkness. Diesel left the bedside light on for me, but my left foot took that out when I got the bright idea to try a bobby pin on the locked handcuffs around my wrists.

I'm going to fucking kill Diesel when I get out of this mess.

Feeling frustrated and exhausted, I grab hold of the bed frame and pull myself up into a more comfortable sitting position. Not that I can get comfortable with my wrists handcuffed to the top of the metal frame.

I repeat—Darius "Diesel" Mitchell is a fucking dead man.

Okay, maybe I can't kill him, but I am going to make him suffer. I just want to get out of here so I can love on my babies and never let go. Rig taking Zander shook me up. My boy's a tough kid, but that's just it. He's still just a kid and he got pulled into club shit. On our way out here from Detroit, he was telling me how well he handled himself. I forced myself to smile and tell him how proud I am of him. And I am, but I'm more scared than anything. I don't even know if that's the right word. I was born into this life, grew up a club kid with little supervision and even fewer rules, and I've seen and done shit that would give grown men nightmares. But my baby being kidnapped was the absolute worst thing I've ever experienced. I don't care that we got him back safely. I don't care about anything except that fucking asshole thought he could take *my* boy and live to tell the tale.

Not that he lived.

A loud bang sounds on the other side of the closed door. My heart skips a beat and I jump from my spot at the head of the bed. The darkness makes me jumpy. I don't know what it is, but the solitude kind of freaks me out.

The hinges on the door creak as it opens. Light filters in, bringing with it a sort of relief. Two figures appear in the doorway—one large and bulking, and one small and slender—casting a shadow over the bed and most of my body and face. Their bodies are pressed together. The larger body sandwiches the smaller one between himself and the door frame. My stomach drops and my mouth goes dry. I have to push back the hurt and remind myself that while I'm technically his, it doesn't mean he's even remotely mine.

Because even though it's been over two years since I've seen him, I'd know him anywhere. Not many people get to be Wyatt's size, and *nobody* carries themselves the way he does. When he walks, it's with this humble confidence that just radiates, but he's totally void of any arrogance. At least that's who he is when he's sober.

The woman he's with giggles. She fucking giggles as his hands trail up and down the sides of her body. Jesus Christ, the sorry fuck is hooking up with girls now. Grown-ass women don't giggle, and we're too damn old to be fucking around with coeds. The little bitch—not that I'm pissed about having to watch my old man maul a damn teenybopper or anything—flips the light switch, basking the room in a soft yellow light. I cringe, blinking away the spots in my vision. Once I'm able to see clearly again, I steel myself to face the only man I've ever loved.

I clear my throat and snicker when the girl turns to face me. She can't be more than a year or two out of high school, if even. She's your basic bottle blonde with too much makeup and not enough pretty to back it up.

"Oh shit," he whispers.

My eyes travel from the whore to Wyatt. I have to actively work to suck in a breath. His light brown hair hangs down to around his hulking shoulders. He's still beautiful even if he has totally lost that youthful, boyish beauty he used to have. It's been seventeen years since I met this man, but his eyes are the same. The narrow shape makes him look like he's always grouchy even when he's laughing, but the blue-green color is inviting and makes him seem almost gentle—like an enormous teddy bear—even though he's definitely not. I get lost in his eyes just like I do every night as I tell our son and baby girl that I love them. Piper's eyes are rounder, but the color is spot-on, and when she gets mad, there's no doubting who her daddy is. Zander is another story. As he's grown and become more of a man, I see less and less of myself in him and more of his father. Sometimes so much so that it's painful.

Coming back to my senses, I adjust wiggle my wrists to give the pair a little wave. With the brightest, fakest smile I can muster, I say, "Honey, I'm home."

CHAPTER TWO

Wyatt

"Get in the chapel, shitheads," Grady yells from behind the bar. His deep voice startles me from the half nap I had going on. *Fucker.* We don't have Church for another few minutes, but he's trying to step out early so he can get on the road to go see Miss Priss down in the city. That kid's his world, so I get it, but for fuck's sake, let a brother nap.

I pry one eye open just long enough to see that nobody's really moving yet. They know his game, and they're not playing it either. With that knowledge, I close my eye and try to regain some fucking peace. Diesel isn't even back yet from wherever the fuck he went.

It doesn't take long for people to migrate my direction—one set of heavy boots and another set that clicks. Christ, if a chick is heading this way, they're probably going to be fucking yapping and talk-blocking my goddamn nap. Not that this is the best place to catch a few z's, but my place is too dirty to get comfortable in. I need a steady bitch for some regular pussy, a few home-cooked meals, and a little maid service.

"You ready for this?" It's Ruby. I'd know her voice anywhere. It's not exactly soft in tone, but it's gentle while still sounding self-assured in a way that only she can pull off.

The next voice I hear is Pop's. He grunts before using his words and saying, "Never gonna be ready, but it's time."

It's time.

Those two words make my body lock up, my lungs reject oxygen, and my mind go blank.

It's time.

I know it's coming. We talked about it a few months back, but that doesn't make it any fucking easier.

I'm not ready either, Pop.

"Go," Ruby says. Jim grunts again and walks off, leaving Ruby behind. I suck in a deep, necessary breath, and try to get back into the napping groove, but it's no use.

It's time.

"I know you're awake." Her voice is closer now. I give up the sleeping act and open my eyes to find she's hovering over me with a sympathetic look on her face. "I'm your president's old lady for about ten more minutes, so just give me this, will ya?"

I give her nothing, which is about the most I'm capable of right now.

"I'm selfish. I want my man at home with me, and in order to get that, he has to give up the gavel. Because with everything going on, even when he's with me, he's not *with* me. I want this as much for the club as I do for myself. I have my kids—*all* my kids—and my husband for the first time in my entire fucking life. I know you don't want this, Wyatt, but please, please don't fight it."

"You make arguing difficult," I say. She's not wrong, so I have no argument. I just wish it wasn't like this. I wish it wasn't me.

"That's because you know this is right."

She's tiptoeing around the elephant in the room. We both know what she means, but neither of us are willing to voice it. It's fucked enough to admit to myself that Jim's not doing his job. I can't verbalize it to Ruby or anyone else. In our world, that's treason.

The chapel is silent—which never happens.

We've got seven votes in, and it all comes down to me and Trigger. Torque, who's only been out of county for a few months now, just voted yea. Asshole even winked at me when he did it.

The vote has to be unanimous for it to pass. The only way for Pop to leave his seat without a unanimous vote is if he inks out or dies. Brothers don't force a president to stay if he doesn't want to. It's fucking disrespectful. But a big part of me is praying—or begging—that Trigger votes nay and this bullshit about handing me the gavel will blow over. It's not that I don't want it. It scares me. These men are voting to place their lives in my hands, and fuck if that doesn't say something.

"This isn't how presidents go out," Ryan says. His elbows are planted on the table before us, and he's snarling at the finished wood. "But if it gets you off my dick, then yea."

Seven sets of eyes land on mine at once. I try not to fidget or move in my seat. They've voted to make me president. All they need is *my* vote now. What kind of fucking crock is that? I have to vote on my own promotion. Bullshit. If I could, I'd fucking change that. When I throw up my middle finger and growl, "Yea," at the room, I feel like a fucking tool. I'm not an insecure dude, but fuck if this isn't making me feel like my asshole is growing a pussy.

The room erupts with cheers and taunting from my brothers—my men—as I take this moment to absorb what's happening here. I started in this club seventeen years ago as a prospect and worked my way up over those years. I've handled runs, paid off cops, bribed politicians, had more money than I knew what to do with, and have killed in the time since I patched in.

The Forsaken Motorcycle Club is my life.

It's my home.

And now the Fort Bragg charter is mine to protect.

"Pass the kit," Pop says from beside me. The sewing kit gets passed to the head of the table, and Pop and I remove our president and vice president patches, respectively. With dirty, worn hands, Pop holds his patch in front of him and studies it for a long moment. Then he slides it over to me.

A wave of emotion comes over me as I stare down Pop's president patch. With a single finger, I touch it, like I'm making sure it's real. Most brothers keep their patches to remember their time in that position, but some hand them down to the next in line. It's the greatest honor a retiring president can bestow upon the new president.

Everyone in the room has their eyes on us, waiting for my reaction. The younger guys keep their eyes on Pop. His sons—Ryan and Ian—are slowing nodding their heads. Like, somehow, they know this is right.

Grady, Pop's sergeant at arms, has his eyes on me. The expression on his face remains impassive except for the small lift of the corner of his mouth.

"You fucker," I grumble, refusing to meet his eyes. My brothers laugh, but it's not the chaos-driven maniacal laugh I usually hear. It's deeper, a little sad, and maybe even a little hopeful.

I sew on my new patch slowly, careful to make the stitching look good on my leather cut. And I take a deep breath every now and then to stabilize myself so I don't fucking lose it. My hands want to shake, but I don't allow it. The men around me can tell I'm nervous, no doubt, and they don't judge me for it. My unease shows them that I take this seriously, and that means something to them. I know it does, because back when I was patched in to Detroit, Amber's dad was president, but then he patched out of Detroit and into the California Nomads, leaving us with his VP, Rig, to take his place.

Amber.

I fucking hate thinking about that woman, so I force myself not to, which is a lot like trying to ignore a third degree burn.

Rig didn't act nervous. He seemed at ease, like he always expected to take the throne, and it didn't sit well with his men. I was too young and too stupid to understand the gravity of it back then, but I sure do now. My brothers didn't just vote to give me a title—they voted to give me power, authority over their lives, and the responsibility of keeping them alive.

Fuck.

I'm not ready for this.

I've barely finished sewing my president patch onto my leather before Pop stands from his seat and places his hands on the back of the chair. He takes a deep breath, his eyes scan the room, and he laughs.

"First time I sat in this chair, I was still in diapers."

I groan and turn my attention to Ryan, who's grinning from ear to ear.

Three, two, one…

"Going out in diapers too, eh, old man?"

For the first time in almost a year, Pop smiles. It's not a smirk. It's not forced. He's just…smiling. His brows are relaxed, his cheeks are high and pushing up on his eyes, and his chest shakes with laughter. He shakes his head. Not since Pop came to me before Church and told me he was putting in that marker has he looked this chill. Not only was that conversation close to his heart, but everything that followed it was a goddamn consequence of our choice to head out to New York. I don't regret it. I *can't* regret it. Alex was just some girl who got caught up in shit she couldn't handle when I promised Pop I had his back regardless of what the club voted. She's not much older than the kid I almost had, but she's tough, and she's growing into one hell of a woman. Chief wouldn't want us to regret the shit that went down, even though we lost him in the process.

"I'd like to blame your mother for that mouth of yours, but I'm afraid you're all me," Pop says.

"Well, half you and half some hooker you knocked up," Ryan says dryly. He never talks about his birth mother, so nobody really knows what to say. Pop only ever refers to Ruby as his mother, even if she didn't give birth to him. Thank fuck, too, because the whole Ryan and Alex thing would be more twisted than it already is.

"He's your problem now." Pop's got his eyes on me. He slaps the back of the chair and walks around the table to Chief's empty seat at the other end. He stares at it for a long moment before pulling it out and sitting down. We're silent as he gets comfortable. Nobody's sat in that chair since Chief.

When the moment passes, everyone's eyes drift to me. I stare at them for a long time before realizing that they expect me to take the head of the table.

"What? I can't even get drunk first? You fucking assholes." Moving from the VP's chair to the vacant seat to my left takes more effort than I could ever imagine. It's the second most difficult thing I've ever done.

The most difficult thing I ever fucking did was walking away from the only person I was living for.

The rest of Church is terrible. It doesn't even suck. It's not like the time Grady and Trigger pulled a piece on each other. It's not like when Chief died. I have no idea what I'm doing here. I fumble through procedure, trying to lead my brothers—my men—through voting in new officer positions and deciding if Squat is ready to be patched. I'm not a small dude, but I feel like I'm about a foot tall through this fucking meeting. Pop refuses to take any other officer position, saying he just wants to ride until he can't anymore, and after every single person in the room hassles him, we finally move on. I suggest Grady for VP and nobody objects.

To everyone's surprise, Grady raps his knuckles against the wooden table and says, "I want Trigger for sarge."

"You yankin' my dick?" Ryan's eyes are narrowed and his brows are pulled together.

"You're a shithead, you got a loud mouth, and you're disrespectful. You need to chill your temper, and there's no better way to do it than to be responsible for the discipline of your brothers. Time to grow up, son."

It's a bold move, but after a few comments from the brothers, they vote in favor of the nomination. Diesel takes over as road captain, and then we move on to discussing whether or not Squat deserves his top rocker. Bear, Torque, and Grady are hesitant. Torque doesn't really know the guy, and Bear and Grady think he needs more time with the club.

"Every man at this table has a history that brought him here. For Rob, that was Aaron. Aaron died trying to keep our women safe. His death still fucks with Mindy. They got close before he died, and she's made friends with Rob now. He's hurting, but he shows up every day, does his part, and doesn't bitch. I don't doubt his heart," Ian says.

"So, take another vote," Torque says.

We do, and this time, everybody votes in favor of patching the little fuck in.

"I'll get his top rocker, Pres," Pop says from the other end of the table.

"Asshole," I say and shake my head. He just *had* to call me that. "Somebody get Squat in here. I want this meeting over with as soon as fucking possible."

CHAPTER THREE

"This party is shit," Duke says. He tips his head back and looks over his shoulder at his old lady who's breastfeeding their baby across the room. Not gonna lie—Nic's tits have gotten real nice since she had Robin. Not that I've been looking since Duke caught me eyeing 'em a few weeks back. There's a lot of shit brothers don't care about, but respecting their old ladies is mandatory.

"You're the one who's turning this place into Chuck-E-Cheese," Grady grumbles with a sideways glance at Duke.

"I'm just saying. We didn't plan anything."

Neither Grady nor I make a move to get up. The clubhouse isn't dead, but it's not hopping either. It's a weird night, and nobody knew Jim was going to ditch the gavel today, so we weren't prepared for anything.

"Don't worry about it," I say and finish off the beer in my hand. "We'll have Ruby get something together."

"Except she's not the pres's old lady anymore." Grady shoots me a taunting grin. I do my best to ignore him. I know what he's getting at, and I have no interest in going down this road with him.

"And on that note, I'm gonna go find some pussy."

Standing from the table and surveying the room, I spot two lost girls behind the bar. One is bare at least from the waist up, and the other has just a bra on. They're quietly talking to one another while wiping down the bar top. With the snap of my fingers, I have their attention, and with the crook of my finger, I have the new girl coming toward me. I haven't had her yet—don't even know her name—but she's here and she's willing, so she'll do. Anything to get Amber out of my head.

Grady is a real fucker for bringing her up. It's not like I can go more than a few hours without thinking about her as it is. I'm on autopilot as I grab a hold of the bitch in front of me and take her mouth. I can't really feel her touch even though she's trying to get her hands on every inch of my skin that she can. My body is here in the clubhouse, but my heart and mind are back in Michigan in a grassy field watching a girl give a mean old man the dirtiest look I've ever seen.

Amber Wallace isn't the love of my life.

She's not the one who got away.

She's not my old lady.

She's my everything, and if I weren't so used to admitting that to myself, I'd feel like the biggest fucking pussy.

I keep my eyes mostly closed as I devour this bitch's mouth and palm at her ass. My gut twists the closer we get to my room. It's like a lead balloon that's getting bigger with every step. The woman in my arms is soft to the touch but not nearly soft enough. It's not the skin I miss getting lost in. Her curves are all wrong, and her hair is too straight. Nothing about her feels right, and even though I know I'll be hard enough to pound her pussy once we're naked, I'm not going to enjoy it the way a man should enjoy getting his dick wet.

Regret is a powerful emotion, and it doesn't get any easier with the passing of time. If anything, it just gets worse. Days go by, and you don't chase after her. Then weeks. Months. And finally years go by, and no matter how much you want to drop to your knees and rip your own fucking heart out of your chest for breaking the strongest woman you've ever met—you don't. Because some mistakes can't be fixed, and there's no going back.

Not everybody gets a happy ending, and I've had to learn to live with that. Even seeing half my brothers get hooked up with old ladies isn't enough to make me seek out mine. I've been down that road more than a time or two, and it always ends with me in a two-week detox. It was fucked enough when I was VP, but as president, I can't be going off the fucking rails for some pussy that rode somebody else's dick and walked out on me over a decade ago.

I've got the chick pressed up against the door to my room when the lead balloon in my stomach feels like it explodes. Amber isn't some pussy, and I've never believed she cheated on me. I just don't know how to make any of it any better. I can't make it hurt less. I can't make myself forget her. I'm rendered totally inept when it comes to moving on from Amber Wallace.

"Baby, what's wrong?"

I hear the bitch I'm mauling speak, but I ignore her. There's nothing wrong except for the fact that she's not my old lady. She's not the woman I'd spent four successful hours not thinking about before Grady brought her up. She's not the woman who once told me I'd make a great president. She's not my fucking body and soul, so I ignore her because she's nothing more than a warm wet hole I can drown in for a little while to numb my self-loathing.

My hand wraps around the door knob, but I stop. It doesn't happen often, but sometimes I just don't feel like having sex. With one hand, the nameless whore grabs at my dick, and the easy fuck jumps right up. Well, there goes the whole being good thing. Her other hand covers mine on the doorknob and we tumble into the room. She giggles, and if I didn't already feel like an old-ass pervy fuck, I sure do now, and then she turns on the light. I've barely adjusted to the light in the room when a throat clears from the other end.

My heart stops immediately.

My lungs won't work.

"Oh shit." The words leave my mouth before I even realize I've said anything. I'm still processing what I'm seeing.

Amber Wallace.

My old lady.

My entire fucking world is in our bed. An angry scowl drags her brows together and has her mouth pinched up in the corner. Her reddish-brown hair is up in a messy bun that's half fallen off her head, and her green eyes are trained on me like I'm something disgusting she stepped in. I don't deserve that look, and it pisses me off. I don't deserve the goddamn gift of having her here—even if she is pissed—and I sure as fuck don't deserve to have her anger. I threw all that shit away a long time ago.

In a matter of moments, the last twenty years of my life flash before me. Everything from my bullshit teenage angst to the first time we kissed to the last time I had her naked and writhing underneath me. I work to fight the instinct to rush to her, claim her, and never let her go. I can't go down this road again. I'm not Fort Bragg's number two. I'm their president, and that means I have to keep my shit straight no matter how much I want to spend the next two weeks repenting for my sins, both of us naked and greedy for one another.

Amber's arms are pulled up above her head, locked around the metal headboard with a pair of cuffs. She wiggles her wrists and grins at me, never breaking eye contact. She says, "Honey, I'm home," like she means it. But I know her better than to assume she's really back. Not that it matters, because she never really left me. She's always been here—in my heart—right where the crazy bitch belongs.

CHAPTER FOUR

Wyatt's eyes harden in an unfamiliar way, and he tilts his head to the door as he says, "Out, bitch." His eyes don't leave mine, but I know he's not speaking to me. Not that it would matter if he was, since my ass is handcuffed to this fucking bed. The stupid bitch doesn't leave. My hating on her has nothing to do with her. It's purely about the man before me—the man staring at me with such indifference that I feel even less significant than I did back in the day when he was screwing anything with tits.

"Maybe you're hard of hearing, but my man told you to get the fuck out." I bark the words at her but don't take my eyes off of Wyatt. His eyes widen but just barely, and if I hadn't spent so many hours over the years just looking into those beautiful eyes, I wouldn't notice it. Before I let myself absorb the change in his behavior, I turn my attention to the woman at his side. She looks so angry that I think she's going to charge at me. Her nostrils flare, her eyes bug out, and she's breathing heavy. She thought she was going to spend the night with the VP but is getting her ass kicked to the curb.

"And who the hell are you?" she snaps.

A slow, steady warmth fills me as my lips curl up into a smile and I say, "I'm his old lady."

When Wyatt doesn't correct me, her shoulders slump and she slinks out of the room. She's barely cleared the doorway when he slams the door shut and locks it. He's acting strange, and I don't understand it.

We stopped being us before Zander was born, but we've seen each other a handful of times since then. Each time begins and ends the same way—with my man walking toward me and scooping me up in his arms. He takes my mouth and palms my ass and tells the entire world that his old lady is home. And then he drinks a bottle of whiskey, fucks me until I pass out, and when I wake up, he's higher than a kite. He doesn't talk to me until he's good and wasted and can't remember anything. He always asks about Baby Z and I always tell him about our son and with tears in my eyes I tell him I want him to know our boy. And then he does a couple of lines, downs more booze, and promises me that we're going to be a family.

And it's over when we start fighting because he starts making unreasonable demands that don't make any sense. And no matter how much I want my son to have his father, Wyatt ends up detoxing out of town in a cabin somewhere, and I always hope he's going to reach out once he's clean and sober, but he never does.

"You think this is cute?" he says with a nod to the handcuffs.

"Yeah, don't you?" The sarcasm in my voice can't hide the shakiness. There are a few things I don't doubt—that the two best people on this planet call me mom, and that this flawed man loves me, the kind of true, deep love that consumes you, and that I love him impossibly more than that. Except now, in this moment, I'm questioning that second one. We don't engage in small talk. Actually, we don't really *talk* at all. We've never needed to. We were always better at showing how we feel through touch.

"What do you want? I got shit to do," he says without an ounce of emotion in his voice. I have to swallow all the love and hate and fear that threatens to spill out of my mouth while he's so…blank.

"Well, uncuffing me would be a solid start." I nod my head at the table where Diesel left the key. "Your guy Darius seems to think I don't uphold my end of a bargain."

"Diesel cuffed you?" A smile graces his face, and it's the first time I've seen it since we conceived Piper. I miss his smiles. Truth is I miss everything about him except his not-so-fucking-little chemical dependence problem.

"No, asshole. I cuffed myself. Thought it'd be fun to hang out in your cum stains for the evening."

He moves one foot in front of the other so quickly that I don't realize he's thrown himself on the bed. He's hunched over, his fists and knees planted in the mattress. Wyatt is every bit a predator with his narrowed eyes, calm, even breaths, and taut muscles that would intimidate most men and excite every woman on the planet.

"In this clubhouse, with this club, you are *my* property. I don't give a fuck where you go or what you do, but goddamn it, woman, when you're here, you're gonna act right."

Oh. Fuck. No. My heart rate speeds up and a thin sheen of sweat covers my forehead. I feel gross having been stuck here for hours, but more than that, I just feel pissed off.

"I may be your property, but you represent me, and no man of mine fucks some whore in *my* bed."

He inches closer, his fists flanking my legs. His eyes have a laser focus that sends a shiver down my spine. It doesn't matter how much of a jackass he is—he still affects me the way he always has.

"Bitch, you need to watch yourself." His words are laced with an angry warning that might scare other women, but I was raised by a man far less loving than Wyatt, so they fall short with me. My man knows how to fight, but I think he's forgotten who taught him how.

He continues to crawl up my body. I purse my lips and wait until my knee is perfectly aligned with his amazing dick. I fight the urge to tell him what I'm about to do is going to hurt me more than it's going to hurt him. I don't make a habit out of lying to people, so I'm not about to start now. In all honesty, I've been fantasizing about this for years.

I take a deep breath and clear my mind of every reservation I have about sending his ball sack up his ass and throw my knee straight into his dick, but he's picked up on the move. In the last second before I make contact, he shoves his huge-ass arm in between my legs, forcing my knee to the side and into his hip instead. He palms my ass, giving it a rough squeeze, and settles his undamaged family jewels in between my legs. His lips hover just an inch above mine, and his hair falls in my face. My wrists ache under the strain of my position—half sitting up and half lying down without a meaningful grip of the headboard railings—but I refuse to ask to be let up.

"That's no way to treat your old man." His warm breath washes over my face. He smells of whiskey and cigarettes but nothing else. He can't have had much to drink yet, because his eyes aren't bloodshot and he's not slurring promises of love and devotion that he has no idea how to keep.

God, I just want to stab him with tweezers or something. One day I'd like someone to explain to me how I can love this man so much that my body physically aches to be near him but still want to force him to swallow his own tongue. He's annoying, insufferable, and by far the absolute most difficult man I've ever met. He's going to make me gray early, and that's just going to piss me off even more. Of all the dysfunction in my life, Wyatt Strand takes the cake.

It's on the tip of my tongue—the confession that I'm here to make.

"You teach people how to treat you," I say. In my head, I'm telling him right now about Zander. In my head, he's losing his shit on me because I'm still handcuffed and can't get away. And I chicken out.

"Good thing I taught my son to treat women better than you treat his mother."

My son.

I should have said *our son.* It would have been so easy to just say it. Except for the fact that I can barely breathe at the thought of telling Wyatt he has a fourteen-year-old son. You'd think with how many times I've told him about Zander that it wouldn't be hard to do it now—except for the fact that he's sober now, and he'll remember this time.

"I can't have this conversation with you," he says thoughtfully. His eyes look are so much bluer now and his voice is rougher. The fight blows out of me, and all I have left is the sorrow in the pit of my stomach that never goes away.

"We have to talk about him." There. Effort. "Like, we *really* have to talk about him."

"Talk later, fuck now." Wyatt cups my ass with his hand and kneads. I bite my lip, trying to keep silent, but it's no use. A soft moan escapes me. I want nothing more than to wrap my arms around him and never let go. But I'm still freaking cuffed.

"You're not fucking me with these cuffs on," I say.

He just lifts an eyebrow and smirks in such an incredibly sexy way that I'm left speechless. The few inches that separate us disappears, and Wyatt skims his nose along my jaw. My body buzzes with his touch. It doesn't even matter how obnoxious or difficult he can be. I won't deny him because I love him. Because the only thing worse than loving a man like Wyatt Strand is loving him from afar.

"Baby." The word escapes my lips like a plea or a prayer, I'm not entirely sure which. I want more—so much more—but we really need to talk, and if things keep going down this road, we won't be doing any talking. I tell Zander all the time that history repeats itself if you don't learn from your mistakes, but maybe I should be taking my own advice, because with Wyatt and I—we don't talk, and then when I'm ready to, it's too late. Every single time.

I'm about to open my mouth when my man brings his lips to my neck. It's second nature to tilt my head to give him more room. His tongue drags itself over a vein in my neck, from the bottom of my jaw all the way down to the top of my collarbone and back up again. Every hair on my body stands at attention, reveling in every tiny little touch I get and anticipating the next one. Being touched by him, like this, is the kind of gift that can't be taken for granted.

"What are you thinking?" His breath is hot on my skin.

"I miss you," I say as honestly as I can. "I miss us."

"You left me," he says, reminding me of something I've never once forgotten. "Walked out with your kid and left me." He takes a deep breath and sits up. There's a flash of regret in his eyes, and I can't tell if it's over a history that neither of us really wants to revisit or if this is something new. I don't say a word as he pulls a key from his pocket and leans over me, unlocking the cuffs and freeing me from my prison. I laugh to myself at the thought of those cuffs being my prison. The only thing that's ever really bound me is sitting in front of me with a grim look on his face and a sorrow in his eyes that I don't know I'll ever be able to fix.

On shaking wrists, I push myself up into a sitting position. My wrists aren't bruised or anything, but my arms are sore as hell. Still, the discomfort in my body is nothing compared to the discomfort in my soul. Wyatt messed up all those years ago, but I left. I made the choice to walk out, and even if I can't regret my choice to keep our son safe, I could have tried to mend fences, and I didn't.

"I have to..." I start speaking but can't finish my thought. "I have to tell you something."

The only thing worse than having this conversation is the thought of not having it. If Diesel is the one to tell Wyatt about Zander and Piper, the outcome will be way worse. Tears well in my eyes at the thought. Fuck. I hate crying. If my dad saw me crying, he'd grab me by my shoulders and tell me that there are only three things worth crying over—death, your kid, and running out of whiskey. Then he'd hug me, because no matter how old I get or how little we see each other or whose old lady I am, I'm still his kid. But he's not here. He's at his house with my kids, who only get to see him once a year or so. This might actually be Piper's second time seeing him, with the first being the day she was born. My dad may not show up for much, but he's damn sure been there when his baby is having a baby.

"Babe, just say it." Wyatt's voice is gentle. *Too gentle.* I don't deserve this kind of sweet from him. Part of me wants to start sobbing and play the victim, telling him I'm afraid he'll hate me and how very sorry I am. But that's fucked, and old ladies don't act like that. The club didn't vote me in so I could manipulate my man. They voted me in because I know how to take my hits, and I can do it without acting like a pathetic little bitch.

"I lied to you. When I left—I lied." I suck in a deep breath, hoping it helps calm me some. It doesn't. "I told you what I had to in order to get our son out safely."

Wyatt's eyes bore into mine, completely unmoving, like he's trying to read between the lines but failing miserably. He's smart, though. I know he knows. Somewhere, deep in his heart, he has to have thought about it. Or maybe I just don't want to believe he'd ever buy that I cheated on him. Either way, it definitely doesn't matter, because I left and he never came after me and I never took the opportunity to come home.

Until now.

When Wyatt finally reacts, it's with a simple nod. I lower my eyes, unable to watch his eyes as the wheels turn in his brain. He's working through it all—fourteen years of lies and betrayal all unmasked with a single word.

Our.

"I can't believe a fucking word you say." His words are barely audible, coming out on a whisper. He rubs his hands over his face and stares at the wall behind my head. I can't see the look on his face anymore, just his movements, but it's enough. Every ounce of fear and regret that's built up over the years solidifies in my gut, leaving me with a weight that keeps me feeling like I'm being suffocated.

"You were a volatile drug addict, and you scared the shit out of me. I left because you made it clear that the only way I was going to keep Zander safe was if he was away from you." I let my mouth run with all the thoughts in my head. I don't give a single second's thought to the consequences for this kind of honesty. I've spent my boy's entire life in a lie, and I'm done with that life.

"Stop," Wyatt barks. His voice is edgy, angry, and the muscles in his neck are strained as he speaks. If I don't say it now, I know I won't. So I keep going even though I wish I could just shut the hell up already.

"I begged you to lay off the whores, pleaded with you about the drugs and the drinking, and none of it made any difference. I think I would have lived like that, but then you went and threatened me. You were so fucked up, I bet you don't remember the shit you were spewing, but I do."

He pushes off the bed so quickly that the movement makes me jump. I watch every little thing he does, from frantically looking around the small room to the way his chest rises and falls quickly despite his attempts to slow his breathing.

"I can't do this," he says. He turns for the door, and I know if I don't make a decision right now, then I won't have the option anymore. There's a dangerous aura around him that I remember all too well. His body radiates hate and hurt, all overlapping one another and becoming something entirely different—more desperate, dangerous, and depraved than I've ever seen from him in the past.

And because I'm terrified of what his leaving means, I scramble to get to my feet and clear the bed, and in no time I'm wedged between him and the door. This isn't how it was supposed to go. Not that I'd thought about this a thousand times before. Like the day Zander said his first word, or took his first step. I certainly didn't think about this moment the first time my boy asked about his daddy—back when he was just barely figuring out what a daddy is—and I definitely didn't think about this moment when the stick turned blue and I realized Zander was going to be a big brother.

"You're going to have to, because as much as you hate me, there's a fourteen-year-old boy out there who needs you, and I've fucked up with him enough. I'm not leaving here until you get your shit straight so you can be a father to your son."

When he finally looks at me, I wish he hadn't. I don't see the man I love in his blue-green eyes. A deadness has crept in that worries me. His mouth forms the words *my son,* and no sooner than they're off his lips is his fist flying at me. I brace myself for the hit that doesn't come, but my relief is short-lived. Wyatt's giant fist lands in the wall behind my head with a powerful blow that cracks through the paint and plaster. He leans in, pulls his fist out, pulling sheetrock with it, and does it again. I squeeze my eyes shut and count my breaths. *One. Two. Three.* I know all too well that it doesn't matter how well you know someone, how much you love them. Violence is a part of this world—something I accepted a damn long time ago. It never gets old, though—the awful pain that comes from a set of knuckles to the face.

A guttural scream erupts from him, just inches from my ear, causing me to flinch and try to blend in with the wall behind me, but it's no use. His fist is still punishing the wall, and I'm stuck between that and the closed door. My chest hurts. Every breath is more difficult than the last, and a thin sheen of sweat forms on my skin. I know better than to grab him and try to calm him down. With how charged he is, he'll take a swing without realizing I'm not the wall. If I could take a few hits to get out of the emotional turmoil the situation I've created has caused, I would. But all that would get me is a broken nose to go with my broken heart.

A whimper sounds from my lips. I sound so weak and pathetic that it makes me sick. My man is smart, and he pays attention even when you think he isn't. The whimper and flinching doesn't get past him. He slides his eyes over my face for a long, confused moment before he's back to shaking his head and raging about how awful I am.

Still. I'm not that woman who cowers in fear from anything or anyone. I don't fear men. Not even ones twice my size. And I certainly don't cry or whimper or let myself bitch out. I'm Forsaken. I'm stronger than that. I take my hits as they come just like any brother does, and when it's over, I wipe away the blood and move on.

But this isn't like every other time, is it? This is Wyatt, and he's unpredictable. Naturally I'm afraid of him and what he's capable of.

Another lie.

I'm not afraid of him or of being hit. I'm afraid that they represent what I've lost. Fourteen years, a couple thousand months, even more weeks, endless days, and countless hours since we've been us. And it hurts more than any broken bone ever could.

"Fourteen years!" He's moved on from processing the news and has careened right into the psychotic anger that I knew would come. "Fourteen fucking years."

When I don't respond, he screams again. Lunging for me, he grabs me by my shoulders and holds me in place like I'm a rag doll he's about to shake. His touch is gentler than I expect. He's holding back now. I should be grateful that he's going easy on me, but all I can feel is a deep sorrow that I've done this to him. The pain in his eyes, the gut-wrenching sound of his voice—that's all on me.

Roaring out a frustrated, "Fuck," he lets me go a little harder than necessary, and I stumble into the door behind me. I open my mouth to tell him to calm down, but I don't have the chance to. Wyatt stomps to the other side of the room, picks up the lamp on the bedside table, and throws it at the same wall he mutilated with his fist. The lamp cracks and bursts into a thousand pieces just a foot from my head. I squeeze my eyes closed. If I'm not watching, I won't have to see him destroy his own stuff. I have the space to run now, just in case something flies at me, or he lunges at me again, but I don't. Instead, I open my eyes and watch the fallout. I let myself watch his pain and frustration. I don't give myself the luxury of turning away when I catch sight of the wetness in his eyes. He wanted our son so much. Having grown up without a dad and doing a dime in foster care as a small child means my man knows how important family is and what it's like to be without one. He asked me for a family before we knew I was already carrying our boy. Never once did I doubt that he wanted to be a father. I just wish he'd been ready back then. As much as he wants to be a dad—and I know he does—Zander wants a father.

So I *force* myself to watch his destruction. The consequences of my choices unfold around me, tearing at what little bit of my heart I'd thought I'd protected a long time ago.

Unsatisfied with a broken lamp, Wyatt moves on to picking up the bedside table like it weighs nothing and throws it at the cement floor. It cracks and splinters to the point of disrepair, but it's still not enough. His heavy boots stomp the damn thing into the hard floor until all that's left is an unrecognizable pile of broken wood. And this continues with the few items in the room until the mattress has been pulled off the box spring and is tossed against the wall, and the bed frame is so mangled that it looks like it was the victim of a twister. And still, through it all, I don't run.

I'm done running and leaving my man behind.

When he stops tearing the room apart, he stands just two feet in front of me. My fingers twitch to reach for him, but my touch won't comfort him no matter how much I want it to. His chest rises and falls quickly, the sound of his strained breathing loud enough to worry me, and his heart beating so hard that I can almost hear it. Once he calms down, his heart always goes crazy fast from the exertion of acting like a human bulldozer. I guess some things never leave you, no matter the time or distance.

"He's really mine?" The words are so fractured and pitiful that it gets me right in my heart. I could burst into tears right now if that didn't feel manipulative and really fucked. This is Wyatt's time to be upset, not mine.

Every ounce of him.

Of course he's yours.

He looks exactly like you.

I try to say any one of the things I'm thinking, but I get distracted by his cut. Right above his heart where it used to say V. PRESIDENT on a dirt-covered white patch is a different patch that takes my breath away. It's older, more worn, and dotted with a spot or two of dried blood. I gasp as I absorb the meaning behind the patch staring back at me.

"You did it," I whisper as I memorize the stitching of each and every letter on his president patch.

One day, baby, I'm going to be king and you're going to be my queen.

He'd told me wanted the gavel the first time I met him, which was right before he started prospecting for Detroit. Dad had seen him hanging around at club events and parties for a year or so by then. Wyatt was a good kid as far as Dad remembers. I'd never seen him around, mostly because I wasn't welcome at the parties. I was barely Zander's age when I met Wyatt. Mom and Dad would have killed me and Mishy if we'd shown up to the clubhouse uninvited. But that day was a family day. Wyatt got to flirting with me, having no idea the world of hurt he could bring on himself by hitting on the president's fourteen-year-old daughter. I told him he could get in a lot of trouble, but he didn't care. He just fed me that line and said he was going to be prospecting and that I was going to be his. I nearly died when he walked right up to my dad, said a few words, and then took Dad's fist to his face a few times without fighting back.

He got his cut and started working on his top rocker that night.

And almost three years later, after he'd been patched, I was voted in and officially his. Club rules didn't mean much, though, because I've belonged to this man since the day we met.

"Tell me he's mine." I'm jarred from my memories by a hopeful, desperate plea. The only thing I can compare the pain and want in his voice to is my own when Rig had our son. I'd have given anything, hurt anyone, and made mountains fucking move to get my boy back in my arms. And it's in this moment that I know we can make this work. He loves our boy—despite all the time that's passed, he still loves Baby Z.

I nod, unable to speak, and watch as all six feet and six inches of my man falls to the ground. He hits the cement with his knees and holds his torso up with his bruised and bloody fists pushed into the top of his legs. I throw myself at my old man and wrap him in my arms as he tucks his face in my neck. His body jerks in my hold. It's not until my neck is wet and my hair is sticking to my skin that I realize this is another first for us.

He's crying.

My own tears fall, dampening the top of his head, but I don't move.

I just hold him and don't ask him to talk or look at me. I've never seen this before and as cathartic as it is, it scares me how badly I've hurt him. Wyatt doesn't just get upset. He tortures himself with every drug he can find, knowing it's going to send me away. I won't let him fall apart again. If he's this torn up about our son, I can't help but freak out about how he's going to react when he finds out we also have a daughter.

CHAPTER FIVE

"Come on, Gramps. Just one shot?"

I shake my head at Zander begging my dad to let him shoot his rifle. The kid is actually fucking bouncing. All six feet of him is buzzing with excitement over getting to play with Dad's toys. I don't tell him that the rifle in question actually belonged to my mother and was passed down to my sister, Michele, when she died. I also don't tell him I'm the reason Dad keeps shooting him down. No pun intended.

"Boy, do you really think my answer is going to change just because you won't stop fucking asking?" Dad asks him.

Zander's eyes roll into the back of his head, and he blows out a frustrated breath. His big-ass sneaker kicks at the wall behind him in frustration. I taught Zander how to shoot a damn long time ago, but I have my rules. He doesn't get to touch a gun if he's being a little asshole and just generally pissing me off. This morning it was his snapping at his sister and sending her into an hour-long meltdown that pissed me off. An hour later it was his asking Dad to take him to the clubhouse after I'd made it clear that he was staying in this way-too-small-for-four-people house until further notice. Now it's the constant asking that's making *me* want to run away. Not that my dad would let me. Don't get me wrong. He loves me and my kids—Piper has him wrapped around her little finger—but he's not a patient man.

It's been three days since I've seen Wyatt, and I haven't heard from him once. Our moment had been interrupted by Grady—who, last I checked, was Jim's sergeant-at-arms back when he was president, but is now Wyatt's VP. Club business takes precedent. Always has, always will. I wasn't expecting some grand declaration of love and for him to make love to me on the floor next to a thousand splinters from the furniture he broke, but I also didn't expect him to stand up and leave me without even looking back. To be honest, I don't know what I expected.

"Hey, Dad?" I can't believe I'm about to ask my dad to watch the kids again. I've been relying on him too much lately, but I find myself asking even though I know I shouldn't. My dad—Elmore "Thumper" Wallace—is a serious badass. He likes his bike, his booze, and his women, and he's not shy about any of it. I love him, even though he's never really been a hands-on dad, and admire the man greatly. But he's the world's worst babysitter. If it weren't important to me that I see Wyatt tonight, I wouldn't even leave the kids.

The night Diesel dragged me off to the clubhouse, I came home really late to find Dad gone, Piper passed out on the couch with chocolate on her face, and my son in Dad's room with the door locked and some cheap-ass porn music coming through the door. I was embarrassed, for sure, but this is the life of a boy in puberty. I can't tell him to stop doing his business, because as a grown-ass woman and mother of two, I need my alone time or I'm going to kill somebody. I just figure he's like his momma and appreciates a little self-loving. I want to say I'm a cool mom, but it's taken me two years of wigging out to get to this point. Now I only ask that he keep it to himself. Another reason he needs his dad around. The best advice I've given him when it comes to sex is to keep it in his pants, and then I handed Piper off to him and walked away. Needless to say, I think his baby sister is a pretty awesome form of birth control. She's cute all right, and I love her to bits, but holy fuck is she a demanding little terrorist at times. Just like her older brother, she needs her dad, too. They need their dad, and I need a nap.

"Been waiting for you to ask," Dad says. He sticks his thumb over his shoulder and tells me to go.

"Why the hell do you get to go to the clubhouse but I can't?" Zander whines. He seriously whines. He's bigger than half the men I know, and he's starting to grow in facial hair, but he's not a man. He's a little boy who's on his way to becoming the man he think he already is. It's crazy how he straddles the fence between being a child and an adult at times. I just wish I had Wyatt here with me to share these small moments with.

"Because I have shit to do," I snap. I hate losing my patience with him. He just wants to go see his dad. I know that. But his dad knows about him, and he knows where we are. He hasn't shown up. I'm not telling my boy that, so I just don't tell him anything. Elle's told me time after time that Wyatt's changed, but with every passing day that he doesn't come by and meet his kids or contact me, I doubt it more and more. Not that I necessarily want him coming up here unannounced. My eyes slide to my baby girl for confirmation that I really, really don't want him coming up here before I can tell him about her.

"That's crap," Zander says with some serious attitude.

I grab my purse from the kitchen counter and cross the room to where he stands. I could lay into him about mouthing off, because normally I would be pissed about the way he's talking to me. But this time it's different. My teenager isn't being a dick because he can. He desperately wants to meet his dad, and as much as I want that for him, I have to make sure Wyatt's in the right head space for it.

"Hey," I say in the gentle voice I use for sensitive situations like this. "I know you want to see your dad. And I want you to see him—I do. But remember what I told you?"

He doesn't respond immediately, so I wait until he does.

"It has to be the right time," he finally says.

"Yeah. Know why?" I squeeze Zander's cheeks with a big grin on my face. He tries to block me, but he's still not learned to anticipate my moves. "Because it'd be a shame to spring you on him and have him say the wrong thing. I don't want to take him out right when you just get to meet him."

"You're insane," Zander says. He finally manages to evade my love pinches and heads for the living room where his sister is parked in front of the TV watching some godawful kids show that makes me want to drink myself into a stupor. Zander grabs the remote and changes the channel. Half a second passes before Piper's head whips around and she glares at her big brother. I have one foot out the door when she yells, "No!" and I'm running down the drive by the time she's in a full blown fit. Before I can even get into my SUV, the TV is back on her channel and Zander is griping about something or other, but he's doing it in a gentle voice. There's one thing I never have to worry about with him—he's a great big brother even though most of the time he doesn't show it.

Knowing my babies are safe, I head into town to make things right with their father. The drive is longer than I'd like. I have time to think, which I hate, and time to worry about everything from the way I look to what I'm going to say to him. I dropped a six-foot, fourteen-year-old bombshell on him, and now what? I just expect him to be gung ho about being a daddy?

I pull up into Forsaken Custom Cycle's parking lot, having resigned myself to walking into the lion's den in my mom wardrobe. Yoga pants, old-ass tank that's stained from any number of things, worn nursing bra I have no business wearing anymore except for the fact that it's the most comfortable one I own, hair up in a messy bun. I'm a hot mess minus the hot part, and there's no making this disaster look any better. I can't make the "I don't care" look work for me anymore.

The gates to the clubhouse are shut, the black plastic slats in the chain-link closing off the outside world. I honk my horn and wait. A young guy, a prospect, who can't be older than twenty or so, opens the gate just enough to step out. He walks to my driver's window and eyes me but says nothing.

"Hey, I'm here for Wyatt," I say and turn so he can see the Forsaken tattoo on my shoulder. His eyes narrow as he thinks about letting me in. He's being safe, and I can respect that, but the fact that he doesn't know me just rubs me wrong. It's my fault, of course, but that doesn't make it suck any less. Wyatt's been here for over a decade, he's this guy's president, and yet he doesn't know me. This kid should be fearing me. He should know how I like my coffee, what my daughter's favorite stuffed animal is, and how to track down my son when he pulls one of his disappearing acts. But he doesn't.

I need to change that.

"You ever hear of Wyatt's crazy bitch of an old lady?"

The prospect doesn't say anything, but his eyes slide to the open gates behind him like he's looking for help. Leaning forward, I angle my back and point at the large script tattoo I have on my back between my shoulder blades that says my man's name. The kid sucks in a deep breath and nods his head.

"Yes, ma'am. I'm Rink. Sorry about this."

"Don't you ever apologize for keeping the club safe and this place secure." The relief shows in his face. One thing I learned about being an old lady from both my mom and grandma is how to talk to prospects. Some old ladies are real bitches to the boys before they earn their top rocker, and a few are still bitches to them after they're patched. Those women don't stay around long because the real old ladies, the ones with lasting power and a deeply embedded respect for the club and its members, run them off. We're a family—all of us—and we don't treat family like shit. The brothers will fuck with the prospects, but Forsaken takes care of their own, and that includes kids that haven't been patched yet.

Rink lets me through quickly, but I kind of wish he'd held me up longer. The parking lot isn't exactly full, but it's not empty either. There's a red Suburban parked in the far corner, an old Jeep a few spots down, and an old beat-up sedan next to the Jeep. I pull in between the Suburban and the Jeep and head for the door. On the other side of the lot, along the side of the clubhouse, are the Harleys. They're all lined up like the pretty pieces of chrome and leather they are. With the number of bikes that are parked out here, the entire charter must be inside.

Great.

Just what I need—an audience.

The heavy wooden door protests as I open it, and once I've stepped across the threshold, the damn thing slams loudly behind me. The noise catches the attention of the few women on the other end of the room. I recognize Ruby Stone immediately. She's aged a little since I last saw her, but just barely. She's at a small round table with another woman, who's got to be mid-twenties at the most, with medium-brown hair and a small baby bump. The two women are flipping through what I hazard to guess is a baby name book. At the bar is another young woman with long blonde hair that flows down her back in waves. She's drinking a can of pop and chatting with a woman whose back is to me. Still, I know this woman without even seeing her face.

Michele Wallace isn't my favorite person on the planet, but she's not my least favorite either. We haven't talked in years, especially after the shit she pulled with that dude she was seeing, but that doesn't stop the smile that spreads across my face. Her dark-brown hair is dyed a bright red, and she's barely clothed—just like Dad said she would be—but she's still my sister. I don't know if I should go up to her and say hi or ignore her like we've been doing to one another for years.

When she turns around to face the blonde woman, it only takes her a second to look my way and stop mid-sentence. She keeps her attention fixed on me for a long moment before she walks around the side of the bar and takes a few quick steps toward me before she stops. Fear shines in her eyes and radiates in her every step. Another relationship I destroyed with my pride.

"Mishy." I'm pleading with her. My voice is soft and needy, and I hope she still remembers that nickname. I couldn't pronounce her name properly when I was little, so I ended up calling her Mishy, and it just stuck. Right before our big fight, I called her Mishy and begged her not to go off with that dude. She didn't listen, though, and I was so upset, so scared, and so angry for her after the fact that I basically shunned her. The memory haunts me even after almost five years.

My feet carry me to her just as she rushes at me. In no time, we have our arms wrapped around one another and we're holding on for dear life. She's obnoxious and doesn't listen for shit, but she's my little sister no matter what she does. I've been preaching about family and forgiveness to Zander since before he knew what any of it meant. Maybe it's time I start practicing what I preach.

"Ambs," she says into my ear. It's a whisper, if even, and it's pained as all hell. I could pretend to ignore it, but I don't. It feels damn good to have my sister back in my arms. We've both made choices in our lives that have brought us to our respective places—the only difference is that my choices led me to being Wyatt's old lady and hers led her to being a Forsaken lost girl.

Our mother would kill her if she were still alive.

Hell, *I* want to kill her. Dad's tried to get her out of it, pleaded with me to talk to her even, but she won't budge. Michele has her reasons for why she does what she does, but that doesn't mean I have to like it.

"This another one of your little visits?" she asks in my ear. I pull back just enough to catch her eye. She's got circles under her eyes that are too dark to be healthy, and there is a heaviness to them that tells me she's under water right now.

"I'm home," I say.

Shock registers on her face just as angry shouts below out from down the hall. I turn to find Ruby and the woman with her at the table staring at me. Ruby's got a smirk crowding up her mouth, but the other woman looks uneasy with her brows pulled together. Michele lets me go just in time for Ruby to walk over slowly and wrap her arms around me.

"'Bout time you're home," she says quietly. The shouting is still going on down the hall, but we ignore it. Instead, Ruby eyes me curiously as she says, "A king can't function without his queen."

"Glad to be back," I admit, trying to avoid all talk of Wyatt. Ruby may not be the president's old lady anymore, but that doesn't mean she's clueless. In a lot of ways, she's the heart of the club.

"Once shit settles, I'm meeting that boy of yours."

I choose not to ask who told her. The woman who was at the table with her diverts her eyes, giving herself away. If I had to guess, I'd say she's Holly, Grady's woman. Gossip runs rampant in the club, so it's no surprise that word has already spread. The logical chain goes from Wyatt to Grady, and Grady to Holly, and Holly to probably half the old ladies.

I don't even realize I'm giving the poor woman a dirty look until she raises her hands in the air and says, "I was excited. I'm sorry."

I wave her off and head over to introduce myself. It's time I settle in and make damn sure everybody knows who I belong to.

CHAPTER SIX

Wyatt

I lean back in my chair, waiting on Michael to show up. I told him five minutes, and it's been at least that. I take a deep breath and force myself to chill the fuck out. We don't have Church for another hour, so he's got time. The club's in a weird position with Michael. He's not our prisoner, but he's not exactly an ally yet either. And despite his age, he's not some punk kid I can lay into whenever I want. If the shit Michael and Scavo have been shoveling to each other is real, then Ruby's boy is making a bid to take over the Mancuso family. The boy taking over and doing all the shit he's said he wants to do is good for the club, not just Fort Bragg but nationally. We'd be allied with not only Mancuso, but his allies as well, and that can only mean less violence, more peace, and less loss on both ends. This beef between Forsaken and Mancuso has casualties on both coasts.

"Hey," Michael says. His voice is so relaxed and casual that it grates on my nerves. I've got enough shit going on right now. Particularly Amber and Zander and figuring out what I'm going to do there. It's only been a few days, but I'm itching to head out to Thumper's and meet my boy. I know I should wait for Amber's okay on that, but she hasn't reached out.

"Where's Scavo?" I open my eyes and eye Michael standing there in a suit. He pulls on the cuffs of his jacket and rolls his shoulders in an uncomfortable fashion. The kid looks like he's about to break out in hives in the damn thing. Not a moment after I've asked does Leo Scavo walk up behind Michael and invite himself into the chapel, closing the doors behind him. I'm pissed at the world right now, so I check my temper with these guys before it blows what could be a very lucrative and beneficial arrangement for both of our organizations. Scavo sits down in Duke's seat, and Michael takes Grady's.

"Nice monkey suit," I say and give the kid a firm nod. He's still squirming in his seat like a madman.

"Part of the whole being boss schtick, I guess," he says.

Leo nods and follows up with, "If you want to be a thug, you can walk around the city with your pants around your knees. If you want to be a businessman, you wear a suit. And stop fucking squirming."

Holding back a grin, I decide to just get on with it already.

"Forsaken likes to keep club business within the club, but I need to run something by you since it affects Mancuso."

"Okay, shoot," Michael says. His eyes go wide with alarm and he gulps. "But not literally, dude. Just, you know, figuratively."

Leo shakes his head and eyes the table. He's probably thinking the same thing I am—that Michael's going to have to get it together if he wants to take over the family. Nobody's going to take a bumbling kid who's about to crawl out of his suit seriously.

"You guys want Junior to take over, but how's that look if Carlo and Emilio are still around?"

"I was hoping your club would take care of that," Michael says. "We're prepared to lie low until the time is right if you guys don't tie up those loose ends. Way we see it, their debt is to Forsaken."

My hair falls in my face when I nod. It's been getting everywhere lately. I don't know how the fuck it got to be so long, but it's basically shoulder-length now.

"You guys are going to need allies once Forsaken takes out the current regime, and I think I know how we can make that happen." The pair of them sit and listen as I talk through my plan. The club has connections in San Francisco that have ties to New York, and last but not least is Segreti. Until recently, the Segreti family had always cooperated with the club and vice versa. But this shit with the botched hit at The 101 Club and the attack on Mindy is something else entirely. I don't trust most of Segreti's organization, but I recognize the awkward position #boss# is in. His men went rogue, and now he's having to deal with it. Not easy, though. Outlaws don't apologize, and they don't show weakness, so I don't know what the fuck we're expecting from the man. Shit. We might have to cap him after all. I shake my head in dismay. I really do hate having to bury bodies if it can be avoided.

I run through everything from my plan to make Segreti Mancuso's bitch down to how Petrov and those crazy Russian fucks can make shit easier for all of us on both coasts with little commentary from either Leo or Michael. It feels victorious. I've spent months thinking about this shit—how to end the violence, take Carlo Mancuso out of commission once and for all, and what we can do to make sure our shit is safe from here on out. There's only one way I've been able to work it that doesn't end in losing half my charter, and that's by taking the fight back to New York.

"You want to take the club off their home turf?" Michael asks, his brow furrowed.

"We're playing defense out here, and it's getting my men killed and their women hurt. I'm fucking done. I need the boys to vote on it, but if they do, we'll head out once we know Carlo's out of Rikers."

"That's smart. I doubt Carlo or Emilio will be expecting Forsaken back in New York any time soon. Once Carlo is released, it's not going to take him long to figure out the mess his nephew's caused."

"You got the heart for this?" I ask, my eyes trained on Michael. I've never had a dad, so I can't say I know how I'd feel if I were in his shoes. Can't be easy, though. "Carlo fucked over Jim's woman, scarred up her kid. As far as I'm concerned, they have every right to take him out."

"My father isn't a kind man. He's prideful and mean. He won't let his men know that the order to take Alex out didn't come from him. He'd have to admit he failed as a leader and let an arrogant prick take control while he was locked up. He'll lose the family regardless of anything else if he lets that be known. I want to believe he'll leave her alone, but I can't take the chance that he won't."

"I need to know before I take this to my brothers that you're on board with this, Michael. I need your word that you'll let us handle your father."

"You know, back in Brooklyn, Alex used to tell me that she didn't want me taking the Omerta. Because then I'll belong to *the family* and not to her family. I don't think I understood how much that upset her until now."

"That a yes or no, kid?"

Junior's face hardens, his expression unreadable. He's staring down at the table, watching his wrists as he rotates them in slow circles. I don't envy this boy or the decision he's having to make. Even if he won't be the one pulling the trigger, he's still promising to stay out of the way when it happens. It's a big deal to ask a son to let his father die.

Zander.

God, this kid is barely old enough to drink and he's faced with this shit. If it were me or my boy...

"My sister is my family. She and my brother...they have to be kept safe. I don't want to be the one to take him out, but I will if I have to."

The tension in the room is high, and it's mostly coming from Michael. We don't talk for much longer. There's really nothing else to say. They're both on board with the club helping them gain some traction in New York, and they'll in turn help us end this war once and for all. Taking out Carlo and Emilio doesn't guarantee us peace, but if we play our cards right, it will secure us a foothold with the Italians that we desperately need in order to keep the threat to my brothers and our families as minimized as possible. If executed correctly, this plan will get Michael and Leo the necessary numbers to overthrow any lingering loyalty the Italians have to his father.

"Closed door meetings with the Italians. Should I be worried?" Diesel strides into the room just as Michael and Leo are walking out. His expression is guarded, his shoulders are hunched, and he's got his hands shoved in his pockets. I don't like it. Not one bit. My brothers don't walk around all apologetic and shit unless there's a damn good reason for it. I seriously can't take anything else.

"We need to talk, Pres," he says, shutting the door behind him.

"You shoot somebody you weren't supposed to?" He grimaces at my comment. He. Fucking. Grimaces. And ain't that some shit. If it were Ryan coming to me with this shit, I'd be worried. Even with Grady, who I trust enough to have made my VP, I'd be jumping down his throat. That's one reason they don't get along—they're both hotheads and way too much alike. But Diesel—he's solid and steady. But something's happened, and now I actually am worried that he's shot someone. He did disappear for a week fucking straight without a goddamn explanation. I didn't like it, but it wasn't my club at the time, so I let it go.

"Need your word you're gonna let me say what I have to, and then you can lay into me. But you gotta let me get this shit out first."

"What the fuck have you done?"

"Your word, Wyatt." He's not asking. This is a demand, but I trust my brother. Regardless of what he has to tell me. So I give him my word and wait for him to start talking.

"Rig's dead." Gone is the evasive, apologetic bullshit, and in its place is an anger I don't expect. It takes me a minute to even register what he's said. *Rig's dead.* As if waiting for me to get with the program, he nods his head and continues. "Your old lady's close with Elle. They vacation together and shit. Kids call her auntie. Few months back, Amber hires Elle to find Rig. Woman puts a fucking bounty on his head from coast to god-damn coast. Few months pass and he's desperate. Takes your boy on a little camping trip. Before you lose your shit, remember that he's fine. He was never hurt."

"How did he die?" It's all I can get out. The only thing I can fucking think about. Rig got ahold of my boy. All these years I've tolerated him when he's come to town. All this time and he's known my kid. The thought of my son learning a single fucking thing from that pussified bitch makes me sick to my stomach. There's so much I was planning on teaching him, so much that I wanted him to learn. Like how to fix up a car, how to shoot a gun—everything a dad should teach their son about life. And I threw away every single day of the last fourteen years so I could shove shit up my nose and drink until my insides fucking rotted. It doesn't matter how much I hate Rig. I hate myself more.

"Asshole had a gun on your kid's head. Amber took him out with three to the gut, one to the arm, and one in the chest. Never seen a woman so mad before."

I try to speak but find that I can't. I want to know where this happened, how it happened, where Zander was before Rig got his hands on him, why Amber wasn't watching him better, and how my boy dealt with that fucking prick pulling a gun on him. I want to know everything, but I'd rather ask my woman than my brother. She sure as fuck didn't lay any of this shit on me the other day.

"I was there. Elle got the call from Rig about exchanging cash for your kid, and I made a judgment call. Right or wrong, I made my choice. We don't have enough men to keep our shit safe out here, let alone sending them to fucking Michigan and leaving our families behind to be sitting fucking ducks. As far as I could see, as long as Rig thought he'd make it out alive, Zander was safe. The minute I go to the club, Rig realizes how bad he fucked up, that he's not getting the money, and the boy is dead."

"The boy?" It's all I can say. The only fucking thing I can think is that this asshole just had the nerve to call *my son* "the boy" like it's fucking nothing. Like he's fucking nothing. I shove my chair back and fly across the table without another thought.

CHAPTER SEVEN

"We good?" I look around the room and wait for confirmation that nobody else has anything to say. They all stare at me with bored expressions. Except Diesel. He's sporting a black eye and a broken nose. He doesn't look bored. He just looks like he got his ass tore up.

He did.

Might not have been fair for me to jump him, but I did, and I'm still too fucking pissed to feel bad about it. Not only did I have to hear that shit from D once, but I had to make him repeat it to the club. It's club business whether it's personal or not. Church ran long for exactly that reason. My brothers needed to know, and some of them were pissed, some understood, and some—like me—were ready for a fight. All I could think the entire time was *this is why we don't allow guns in Church.*

I nod my head and smack the gavel down on the worn table. A strip of wood's been replaced in the table, right where the gavel normally lands. Forsaken brothers have spent hundreds of hours at this table over the years. It's not the original table they had in this room. Rage broke that sucker back before he was president. His old lady, Jim's mom, replaced the original with this one, and though it's seen its fair share of wear and tear, it's held up well. Just like Sylvia Stone herself—at least as far as I've heard—it's sturdy and unflappable. The woman survived more hits than I care to remember and went down with some serious fight. That third time the cancer came knocking, though—she just couldn't beat it. According to Ruby, Rage was never the same once he lost his woman.

Fuck.

His woman.

My woman.

My mind automatically goes to Amber and that bombshell she dropped on me. I guess I'm being a pussy. It wasn't much of a surprise. Somewhere in my heart, I knew it all along. Mugs and I never spent much time apart, and when we were apart, I was with Rig. Not only would it have been improbable for her to have cheated with him, but with how often she rode my dick bare, the odds were on me being her baby's daddy.

But I'm a fuckup who'd snort anything he could get his hands on back then, and that bullshit lie she fed me about not being the father was easier to believe than the idea that she just didn't want me anymore.

I force myself to close out Church and dismiss the boys before I slip back into my thoughts. Once I'm alone in the room, I close my eyes and remember what it was like to have my woman by my side. She was always so opinionated and a total hard-ass about everything.

The timer tells us the test is ready, but neither of us moves to go look. Amber's got watery eyes, and her already pale skin is clammy and cold. I hold her in my arms, dying to know if she's pregnant but fucking terrified to find out. Right now there's the possibility that shit will go on as normal or that everything is going to change. Once we look and we know, that possibility is gone. Fuck. I don't even know why I'm getting so fucked up about this.

"I can't look," she says. So I tell her I'll look because I'm a man and men do shit like that for their women. Even if looking is goddamn terrifying.

I eye the white plastic stick that sits on the edge of the sink and make out the results. One line for not pregnant and two for pregnant.

And there's two very distinct blue lines in the results field.

Two lines that tell me we're no longer just the two of us… we're three people now. Me, my old lady, and our son. Because fuck all that girly shit. I shoot man sperm.

Our fucking son.

Goddamn, it feels good to think that. It feels good to have something that binds me to Mugs.

"Well?" she whines.

I laugh quietly to myself, selfishly enjoying this moment where I'm the only one who knows that we're having a baby.

"Well, your ass is probably going to get fat." I laugh so hard at her reaction—a mix of excitement and fear and irritation at my little comment.

"Come on, momma. Let daddy show you how excited he is," I say as I trail soft kisses up and down the side of her neck.

I actually told her that her ass was probably going to get fat. Shit. I'm surprised I didn't lose a nut sack in that moment. Fifteen years and a kid later and she still looks damn good. Curvier but somehow even more beautiful in ways I couldn't have predicted. Like her fuller hips, larger breasts, and rounder face. As a teen, Amber had a beautiful face, but it was all sharp angles and big eyes. I barely got to touch her the other day—well, at least not the way I wanted to—but she felt thicker, fuller, more womanly than she had in the past.

My mind wonders around in my memories, clinging to some longer than I'd like and ghosting over others that I'm desperate to have a firmer hold on. It's just penance, I guess. I wasn't a good old man and couldn't bring myself to put her first. She was right to leave me and take our son with her. I just hate that the guilt and self-loathing can't chill long enough for me to enjoy even a small non-painful memory. But even those are laced with regret and sorrow. I can't seem to shake the shitty feeling no matter how hard I try. I think of how Amber's belly grew, and how with it, I grew into a man I'm ashamed of. I wanted to be a good brother, to be deserving of the patch, but all I did was fuck up at every turn.

Everything around her fades out, and the only thing that exists in my entire universe is my woman. She's half-angry and half-I-don't-even-know, but she's here and she's in my bed. Her naked body rests beneath mine, freshly fucked and gasping for breath. Her eyes are focused on the ceiling above her, and no matter how I touch her, she won't look at me. Since she came, she's been somewhere else. I want to make the last ten—or is it eleven—years better. I want to erase them and be there with her and our son. I want to be a better man.

"Stay," I say. My voice is quiet, afraid of scaring her off. I feel like we've been here before, but what the fuck do I know?

I've run through enough coke in the last week that I could've financed my own goddamn war if I wanted to. I won't, though. The only thing I want—no, need—is lying underneath me, sated and perfect.

"You're high," she says back. It's simple but heavy. She isn't pointing out the obvious—she's telling me why she can't stay. And fuck if I can't let that be the reason she leaves me again. My gut feels like it's being chopped up into tiny pieces, and the buzzing behind my eyes intensifies. There's this sweet spot with coke and whiskey where everything is perfectly numb. The world actually buzzes. But one extra sip, one too many lines, and it's all shot to hell and you end up in oblivion. I think I'm there now. Amber won't stay, and it makes no sense. I'm here, so this is where she belongs. My vision blurs as I stare into her distant expression. There's a lot going on behind her green eyes that she won't talk about. Maybe she wants to come home, but she's afraid. Or maybe she's moved on. Maybe she just needs convincing.

"Stay."

"And what does that look like?"

I can't find the words to answer her right now, so instead, I move a hand between her legs to show her how focused I am on getting her home permanently. She gasps, her back arches, and her eyes finally lock in on me. My beautiful woman is finally looking at me, and all I can think in this moment is how I want to start over. How I want a thousand forevers with her. How I can't let her leave again. So I kiss her, forcing her to pay attention to me. She doesn't fight me. She just wraps her arms around my lower torso and slides them down to my ass. She squeezes each cheek and bucks into me. I can't feel anything—or I thought I couldn't—but I feel her touch. I feel her lips and her tight hot cunt getting primed for me. Everything in me tells me this is right. We belong together, even if together we're fucked up and I can't stop doing stupid things around her. We're a family, and we need to be together, and the best way to make that shit stick is to grow our family.

I slide into her quickly and without wrapping my dick. She murmurs something against my mouth, but I don't give her the time or space to get the words out. She probably noticed that she's taking me bare, and fuck, I almost forgot how goddamn euphoric this feels. When I finally remove my mouth from hers, I replace it with my hand. She tries to bite my finger, but I use my palm to keep her jaw shut. She's too beautiful not to have a hundred babies with. Maybe not a hundred, but definitely more than one. I still need to meet my son, but he's perfect. I already know that.

"Gonna fuck you bare until you give me another son. You can't tell me I want this because I'm jacked, because it's not true. I always want you. Every ounce and every fucking breath. And I want more of you, more of us, and another baby. You gonna give that to me?"

I reach around and slowly slide a finger into her ass. Her eyes roll back in her head, and she goes stock-still. I rotate my hips, nice and slow, and breathe heavily into her ear. My hand on her mouth moves down to her clit, and even though it's fucking challenging to do without falling on her, I manage to twist her swollen nub in just the right way.

"Tell me you want this."

"Oh fuck. I want it."

Her words come out on a scream that barely makes any sound. She's losing her breath, and her heart rate has spiked. I might not let her out of this bed until I get my way.

I scrub my face clean of the memory. I'm pretty sure I fucked her bare for a month straight before I ended up detoxing out of town. That one month of incredible fucking bliss was the last time I saw her until the other day. Every memory from that month came back to haunt me. One stupid idea after another assaults me every night as I try to sleep. I want to see my son, but the idea of how disappointed he might be does a number on me. Maybe I'm uglier than he expects. He probably takes after his mom. I might not know how to talk to him, or I might say the wrong things. Every little what-if leads me back to this paralyzing fear of fucking him up.

Fuck.

The wooden doors to the chapel squeak as they move. I open my eyes to find Jim standing in front of the now-closed doors. He's staring down at me with a blank expression on his face, and he says, "The fuck you still doing in here?"

"Thinkin'," I say.

"Takes a lot of effort, don't it?"

"Pretty sure I'm gonna meet my kid and fuck him up." I've always been an honest guy, but if I weren't talking to Jim right now I'd feel like a fool.

"Heh. His mom's had him most his life, so the big fuckup's will be on her," he says and sits in my old seat beside me. It's a strange role reversal I'm still not used to. He might be right, and maybe I won't have much of an impact on the kid. My stomach sinks at the thought. Fuck. I don't know if I'm coming or going anymore, and that little memory of the last time I'd seen Amber isn't helping. I was so trashed that it's a damn good thing my boys weren't up for the task. I've already fucked up one kid.

"Hey," I say in a desperate attempt to change the subject. "New York. You thought about it?"

Jim's face falls, but just a little. He might be softening up as he ages, but he's still a mean fucker.

"You're the boss. It's your call."

"And if I take a vote?" I ask, prodding.

"Then you'll find out my answer then."

He gets up and leaves me, once again, alone in the room and alone in my thoughts.

I need to get the hell out of here.

CHAPTER EIGHT

Walking out of the chapel and heading down the hall for the bar, I get distracted by the partially open doors to the palace. The place isn't as bad as it could be, but it's still a fucking mess. A reflective circle shines on the ceiling in the corner of the room. I follow the light down to a mirror that sits on the banquet table at the far end of the room. Fuck. I take two steps into the room, focused on the two lines of white powder that sit on the reflective surface. There was a time when Amber's being here would have me calling up my guy to get me through her visit, but I can't do that now. I got nine guys who depend on me to keep them alive. The easiest way for me to fuck up that trust is to fall back into old habits that put them at risk.

A lost girl, Julie, hangs out on one of the chaise lounges. She's got a cigarette in between her index and middle fingers and a magazine in her hands. She's hot, been around a damn long time, too, so she knows how it's always been around here. She's been there when I've fallen apart and Jim's hauled my ass up to the cabin to detox. She's seen Amber come in, tear me up, and leave me empty. Julie's seen it all.

"Hey, babe," I say with a nod.

She puts the magazine down and takes a pull on the cigarette. The heavy makeup around her blue eyes makes them really shine. She's a good woman. I'm gonna need her on my side now.

"Mr. President," she says with a smile. She takes one more drag from her cigarette before putting it out in the ashtray behind her. I head right for her, barely taking note of the tiny little shorts and tank top she's wearing. She meets me halfway. It used to be that I'd watch the way her legs move, if the shorts ride up or not, and eye her tits as she comes toward me. But in this moment, I keep my eyes on her face.

"Need your help, Jules." She doesn't stop until she's less than a foot away from me. My hands find their way to her hips. "I gotta keep my head right."

"Your old lady's back," she says with a nod. Her smile falls and she says quietly, "With your son. I bet he's a real lady killer."

I bite back from saying the first thing that comes to me. I haven't seen him yet, so I wouldn't know. Fuck. Does he even ask about me? Does he care? Did Amber tell him about the other day? God, he must be fucked up inside if he knows I know and I haven't seen him yet.

I'm not prepared for this shit.

"Sorry."

"Nothing to be sorry about," I say. "Just help me keep this place clean, yeah? Nothing but bud and booze."

"She back for good?"

I don't know.

She says she is, but she's said that before. Then I went and fucked it up and she's gone back to Detroit. I should have tried harder, but how long do you chase after someone who doesn't want you?

"That's none of your business, bitch." Amber's voice, sounding mean as hell, comes from behind me. Jules tenses in my arms but doesn't move immediately. I take a deep breath, trying to check my temper. At least in front of Jules. I disrespected Amber enough in front of other women in the past, and I won't do it again.

"We're still buds," I say to Jules. My voice is low, but she hears me. Her eyes flash a silent *thank you* before she steps out of my grasp and walks around me. When I turn around, I find Amber propped in the doorway, hands on either side of the frame. As long as it doesn't get physical, I'll allow her this show of strength, and because Jules knows what Amber means to me, she'll put up with it. Jules comes to Amber, looks her straight in the eye, and says, "Ma'am."

Something flickers in Amber's eyes. I can't tell if it's anger or not. She's not one to back down from a fight, though, so there's no telling what she's thinking. Even after all these years, I still can't predict what this crazy bitch is gonna do.

"You don't ask my old man about me. You don't look at my old man. You don't talk to him unless he speaks to you, and you sure as fuck don't let him touch you. He may be king, but I'm his fucking queen, and I don't share what's mine."

"Yes, ma'am," Jules says firmly.

"Let the others know I'm back and I'm not going anywhere. You don't know me, but you're about to get to know me real quick. You're going to get to know my son, and you're going to know your place and stay the fuck in it. We clear?"

"Yes."

Amber moves out of the way and lets Jules pass without another word. I don't say anything about the exchange. I don't need to. I stand in place, letting it all sink in.

She's back.

She's taking her place by my side in the club—exactly where she always should have been. I want to believe it. I want it all to sink in, but it just doesn't. Not yet. So many times she's left and come back, and I've let myself think it's for real this time. And every time it's not. Every time she just leaves again, and I'm here. And I'm dead until she returns.

Amber moves into the room, shutting and locking the door behind her.

"You touched her." Her tone has taken on an impossibly angry edge to it. Before, she sounded authoritative, if not annoyed, but her voice is darker now.

"What are you doing?"

"If you don't want your son, just say so." The words come out clearly, but they don't make any sense in my head. I can't even fathom what would make her think I wouldn't want our boy. I've always wanted him. Even when I thought he wasn't mine. Even then. He's a piece of Amber. I'm always going to want every tiny bit I can get.

"I get it. I laid a lot of stuff on your plate the other day. But here's the thing about being a parent—it's not about you anymore. You need time to deal, you do it when your kids are asleep. You do *not* just check out because it gets hard or you're fucked up."

Amber's angry voice softens, like something in her is breaking. Little pieces of the walls she's built up over the years crumble right before me. Her eyes well up with unshed tears. My woman is hard as hell. She's not soft like Princess or broken like Nic. She isn't innocent like Holly or naive like Cheyenne. She's not even lost like Elle. She's just hell on wheels, all loud mouth and kind heart. She's bravery and fear and every little bit the protective momma bear I always knew she'd be.

"I want him. I just need time." My heart breaks with a newfound vulnerability I never knew I could feel. Ten minutes ago I was worried about fucking the kid up, and now…I don't even know what I feel now. It's one thing to talk to Jim about this. I can keep the wall up with Jim. I don't have to feel the pain then. This is different. This is Amber.

"You're not listening." She stomps forward in an angry rush. Her red cheeks are flushed with a heartache I haven't had the chance to understand. Her green eyes are wild. Her nostrils flare. Every ounce of me takes notice of her.

"You do not get time anymore. This isn't about you. This is about your son. He wants to know you more than anything in his entire world, and it scares the crap out of me because I can't force you to be the man he needs. But make no mistake about it—my kids come before everything, and that includes you."

My kids?

I can barely move at the thought of someone else fathering her children. Their seed growing in her belly. Sharing the experience of seeing her body change, creating a family with her...

No.

All the things I chose not to be a part of.

"Kids?" It's probably not the right time, but I can't stop myself from asking. The idea of another man with her, inside of her, just tears me apart.

She flinches. It's almost painful how she reacts to my question. Does she know how it's destroying me thinking about her having kids with someone else? Did she think of me and everything we were supposed to have when she had another man's child? How many does she have...two, three? Did she plan them? Is he still in her life?

There are so many questions, and I have no answers. I don't think I'll ever have enough answers to make sense of how she could have another man's child. Not when we'd promised ourselves to each other. Not when she means everything to me.

"We'll talk about that after I decide whether or not you're getting the chance to know my boy," she says with an angry venom that seethes from her voice. If I'm not mistaken, there's a hurt underneath it all that she's trying to hide. She is strength and vulnerability all at once. She is every inch the ferocious mother to our son I knew she'd be. I didn't just fall haphazardly in love with her all those years ago. I chose her because of everything that makes her who she is, but most of all because of this. Because Amber will scorch the earth to keep her loved ones safe. She did it for me once, and in that moment I knew she was and always would be the only woman I'd ever want to mother my children. I've always loved her, but now, as she rips me apart in defense of our son, I've never loved her more.

"You come into *my* clubhouse after fourteen years and throw me attitude about shit you know nothing about, and I let it go." I try to keep my voice level, but it's no use. Everything in me feels like it's exploding all at once. Every ounce of love I've ever had for this woman is fighting its way to the surface, practically strangling me on its way out. My words are all gravel and broken glass despite the passion behind them. Her brows are knit together, her eyes narrowed, lips parted. She's ready to fight, but I refuse to spend any more time fighting with this woman.

Three steps and we're so close that I'm staring down at her with a craned neck just so I can meet her eyes. I reach out, finding purchase on her hip. She jerks back quickly but still not fast enough. This is our dance. We know the others' moves so well that it's become second nature. With my other hand, I pull her flush against me. She stops pulling back and glares up at me with annoyed green eyes that betray her. She likes this. She missed it.

I can see it in the way her eyes lift in the corners as she smiles softly.

"Look at me," I say even though her eyes were already on mine.

"I am," she defends.

"No, you're not. I'm clean. Tell me the last time you've seen me straight." It takes a moment, but then she gets it. Her face softens, and a sad smile graces the most gorgeous fucking lips I've ever seen. "I'm not that man anymore. A couple of years ago you laid that same shit on me you did the other day, and I ran like a fucking coward. Two years before that, five before that. Who knows how many times I've run the other fucking direction because I couldn't handle the thought of fucking things up with you again."

My chest heaves with the weight of my confession. I've spent three days thinking about this—about her, about him—and figuring out what I was going to say when the time came. I thought I'd have a few more days, but here it is. Amber's got to know that I'm in this and I'm clear headed and I can be the man both she and our son need.

Searching her eyes, I try to find some indication that she gets me. That she believes me. I *need* her to trust in me again. Amber's eyes fall closed for a moment before she opens them again and looks up at me with a fear I haven't seen since we stared at that pregnancy test that told us our entire world was changing. There's so much I want to say, but I can't find my voice.

With slow movements, she reaches up and places her hands on my chest, trailing them up to my shoulders.

She reaches up to my neck, and just like a dance we've performed a thousand times, I know what this means. I wrap my hands around the backs of her legs and lift her up. She's still so light in my arms compared to the enormity of her presence in my life. With her legs wrapped around my hips, she presses herself against me as tight as she can and leans in so close that our noses touch.

"You can't hurt him." It's a plea on the tail end of a whisper. "He's so much like you, all big mouth and attitude, but inside, he's just a little boy who's scared his dad won't love him."

A tear falls from her eyes. She pulls the others back quickly, but it's enough. I don't ruin the moment by telling her that he sounds like his momma, even though he does. God, I bet he's fucking beautiful. I've spent hours thinking about what he looks like. I hope I see some of me in him. I just want to know what that looks like. Before he was even born I used to wish for him to be a certain way. I wanted him to be tall and have his mother's nose. I wanted so much for him. But now, I don't even have to wish because whatever he looks like, however he talks...none of it matters. He's perfect. I already know it because he's ours.

He's mine.

"Tell me more," I say.

"He was born on time. Only time in his life he's not been late." Her eyes are closed and she's smiling. She's fucking smiling. It shatters me.

"His first word was something close to *damn.* My fault. He never got sick, still doesn't, even though he'd spend hours playing out in the cold. He doesn't have a lot of friends at school. His mouth pisses a lot of kids off, but it doesn't seem to bother him. Girls are a problem. I've been doing more target practice since he had his growth spurt. Unfortunately, the kid loves guns. He's addicted to video games and pepperoni pizza. His full name is Zander Wyatt Strand, and he's the most infuriating, lovable boy on the planet."

She named him after me.

"More," I demand. I'm greedy. I need everything I can get. The more I hear, the more I crumble in her arms. Very slowly, I lower us to the floor. She tells me his favorite color is red, followed closely by black, because they're Forsaken's colors. She tells me how she's never hidden anything from him, that she doesn't believe in babying children. She tells me all these little things about him that still aren't enough. And when she takes a breath to think, I kiss her.

My lips slide against hers slowly. She nips at my lips hungrily. Her back is on the dirty floor now, and she's bucking her hips into me. My already hard dick aches from behind the confines of my jeans. Everything about this moment feels right. Everything is perfect. Even in this dirty-ass room, it couldn't be anything less than perfect. Using one arm to prop myself up, I slip a hand inside her yoga pants right under her panties. She's natural—always has been—and it's fucking glorious. I'm damn tired of the prissy bitches who are always so perfectly shaven or waxed. I always want to tell them that real men don't give a fuck about that kind of shit.

If your pussy's wet and your legs are spread, we'll hit it. And if we don't, it's not because you didn't wax. But that would require me to talk to them, which tends to confuse things.

But not with Amber.

Never with Amber.

She bucks underneath me, greedy for more. I slide my fingers through her soft, curly hair, and finally, fucking finally make contact with her pussy. Fuck. I've missed this. She wets my fingers before I even part her gorgeous lips. I can't see them—yet—but I know they're wet and shining. Mugs has got this kind of switch that she can turn on at will it seems. My thumb parts her lips and slides up and down her hot pussy before I land on her clit.

"Tell me you missed me." I rub slow, methodical circles over her swollen nub, just barely ghosting the skin with my thumb. Amber sucks in a shaky breath, her back arches, and she moans in need.

"I missed you," she says. Feeling victorious, I press harder and take her mouth again. I pace myself, not wanting this to be over too soon. It's been three years since I've been here with her. Three long years of feeling like a thirsty man in a desert, desperate for a little water. And even then all I got was a sip. Not nearly enough.

One finger—one lucky fucking finger—slides inside of her. Three pumps and then another finger joins it. I watch her writhe beneath me, the walls of her pussy clamping down on my fingers. My lungs pull in a greedy breath as excitement courses through me. I lick my lips in anticipation. I don't want this to end, but she won't hold out for any longer. I can feel it in the way she grips me, in how her back arches, and she mewls softly. Her lips part, gooseflesh breaks out over her entire body, and she trembles. I readjust the angle of my fingers and curl them inside her, reaching that sensitive spot inside her that makes her lose herself every time.

She's beautiful, falling apart like this. Absolutely glorious. Mugs is always so self-contained. Only here, underneath me, does she ever lose herself completely. My eyes are glued to the slack of her jaw, her bulging eyes, and the way her entire body shakes. When it's over and she's coming down, I mourn it. There's so much between us, that only here, like this, are we close to what we used to be.

"Thanks, babe." Amber's voice is stronger than it should be. She should be breathless and wanton, but instead, she's clear-eyed and back to shielding herself with that hard-ass shell she wears to protect herself with. She pulls my stunned face down to hers and licks the corner of my mouth. She kisses me the way she used to—all fire and vulnerability. A quiet, beautiful neediness that has always awakened the pathetic little boy in me who just wants to love and be loved in return. It's every fucking thing I've ever wanted.

CHAPTER NINE

Amber

Just as I come down from the best orgasm I've had in years, my brain finally clears from the lust-ridden fog I'd been in.

I did it again.

I completely lost myself in Wyatt, submitting to him in every way, right down to telling him that I've missed him. It doesn't matter that it's true. It doesn't matter that being with him never feels anything but absolutely right. Only two things matter in this world anymore, and their names are Zander and Piper.

Shit. How long have I been gone? I stormed out of Dad's house with the sole intent of driving out here, giving Wyatt a piece of my mind, and driving right back home. I didn't plan on, nor did I account for, letting Wyatt have me. He and I are like a disease that spreads so quickly that you almost miss it. A few minutes together and next thing you know, we're both ignoring the outside world. And as beautiful as that kind of love is, it's also dangerous. It makes you think the person you love is the only thing that is important to you. It makes you sever old ties and forge new ones—ones that your lover approves of. But I'm not sixteen anymore. I have two babies who—no matter how big one of them may be—need me. They need me to keep a clear head. *This* can't happen again. My heart stabs at the thought of denying myself, but being with Wyatt isn't worth all that it costs. This almost cost me my boy once. I can't let that ever happen again.

"Thanks, babe," I say confidently and wiggle out from underneath him. Wyatt's always been a fucking genius with his fingers. God, I swear that man was given gifts that no earthly being should possess. I stumble to my feet and rush out of the pleasure palace—a room I genuinely hate on principle alone—and head for the front door. I gave Wyatt a piece of my mind, and then I gave him myself, and now I've done more than I came here to do, so it's time for me to get back to my babies.

"Amber!" Wyatt bellows behind me. He's gaining on me so quickly that I almost give in to the gut instinct to run. I don't, though. What kind of old lady runs from her man? I came back here, thinking I would be the vice president's old lady. I'd be taking cues from Ruby. If Ruby runs from Jim, I can run from Wyatt. But Ruby would never run, so neither will I. I represent Wyatt. I won't paint him as either a tyrant or a joke by running from him. My pulse quickens even if my feet don't as he descends upon me.

"Don't walk away from me, woman!"

I stop just feet from the front door. The room is still crowded, with everyone here, including that bitch Wyatt was touching before I barged in. Even worse—Ruby and Mishy are still here. If I act like a petulant child, I'll be hearing from both of them later. Mishy may not be acting in a way becoming of a founding member's granddaughter, but that doesn't mean she's forgotten the code. We were raised with it, it was sometimes literally beaten into us. *You don't disrespect your old man in front of his brothers.*

Thanks for that one, Grandpa. I have to stop myself from rolling my eyes. It's so fucking archaic, but it exists for a reason. Still, it doesn't matter how well I know that. Being barked at and ordered to do something you don't want to do in front of a group that's supposed to respect you, but sure aren't acting like it is no easy task. I hate this life sometimes.

Wyatt walks around me, blocking my body from the front door, and cups my face so I'm forced to look up at him. I gasp and draw back before I can stop myself. That little, tiny show of fear is going to come back to bite me later. Wyatt's eyes search mine—confusion, wanton need, and even hurt flare in them—as he tries to make sense of the last few minutes. I relax into his touch and do the only thing I can. I beg.

"Please not here," I whisper softly. "Outside, baby."

He lets me hang for a long moment before he nods his head in agreement. He removes his hand from my cheek, dragging his thumb against my soft skin as he does, and takes my hand in his. How is it possible for anything that feels so perfect, so right, to be so toxic? It doesn't make sense, but that doesn't make it not so.

My heart takes another hit at that thought. I hate this so much. More than I can explain.

We walk out into the parking lot hand in hand. I try to ignore the eyes on us and just focus on the conversation we now need to have. Wyatt Strand isn't the kind of man who will allow me to just walk away. He warmed me once, years ago, that I belonged to him. And everything that means. I'm not fighting it. I can't. He's mine and I'm his. That's something I could never deny. Especially not with the two incredible kids we've created.

"You running from me?" His deep voice calls at the end.

"I can't do this," I say. I'm pleading now, but that's too bad. I can't bring myself to care. As embarrassing as it is.

"What can't you do? Because it sure didn't sound like you couldn't do this when you were coming on my fingers."

I flinch. Which is so not like me. I don't shy away from a fight, I don't flinch, and I sure as fuck don't avoid confrontation. You can't survive a childhood like the one I had without toughening up a little. And by a little, I mean that by the time I started kindergarten, I knew better than to cry over stupid shit. Dad didn't allow it, and Mom never encouraged it.

I won't do that with my kids.

"I just can't, okay?" Wyatt won't understand, no matter how I explain it. He hasn't had the benefit of actually being a parent to understand. And maybe that's what's wrong with me. I'm unsettled here. Every time I come back to this place, I feel like there's a million things I need to apologize for. I tied to reconnect with Wyatt. I know I did, but maybe I didn't try hard enough. Maybe I could've done more. I could've insisted that he go to rehab or get clean. I could've done so much more than I did, which was run.

"I can't fight with a goddamn ghost. What's wrong with you?" Wyatt's words are harsh. So harsh that a drop of his saliva hits my cheek. I take a deep breath and lock my jaw in place before I fly off the handle. Checking my temper has never been one of my strengths.

"This is our thing, Mugs. I act like an ass, you put me in my place, we fight, and then we fuck and do it all over again."

"Well, maybe that doesn't work for me anymore. Maybe I see this for how toxic it really is." And I rush off toward my SUV to get away. It won't work. I already know that well before he catches up to me.

"Open the gate!" I try not to sound panicked as I shout my order to the prospect who stands guard, but I think I fail miserably. He doesn't even look to Wyatt before moving to the lock at the center of the gate and pulling one side open halfway. I turn to give him a quick nod, but something past him, outside the gate, catches my attention.

My feet still as I try to figure out what I'm looking at. Something looks off, feels wrong, but I can't make out just what. Outside the clubhouse gates is the parking lot for Forsaken Custom Cycle. It's a front for the club's illegal businesses and doesn't get much action. Every now and then the boys will have a big order to fill, but that's usually around the time of the annual parade Fort Bragg puts on to show off its love of Americana. It's basically a big party for bikers and the only time I think FCC actually earns out. So, this time of year, the lot should be mostly empty.

But it's not.

"Fuck, Amber," Wyatt says from behind me. He wraps his arms around my midsection and pulls me to him. I try to shush him, but he just holds me tighter, so focused on this fracture between us that he's ignoring his instincts. He feels it, I know he does. He wasn't raised in the club, but he's had the same training I have—even more, actually.

"Something's wrong," I whisper. I keep my lips as still as possible while I mentally check every car in the lot. There's an old Impala hanging out by the door to the office. I think that's been here for a while now, so I ignore it. It's the black van sitting off to the side with a dude in the driver's seat that bothers me. He's got a paper map open in front of him, and he's trying to figure something out with it. But it feels off. He's parked in a weird spot, not in any space I'd choose if I had to suddenly pull off the road to figure out where I was.

Wyatt's senses kick in. I can feel it in his arms. They tense around me. His breathing slows even as his heart rate spikes. This is my man kicking into warrior mode. One of the first things that made me fall for him was his sense of stillness in the midst of war. I can't even remember what started it, but back in the day, a fight broke out inside of Detroit's clubhouse. Even though my man was just a prospect back then, he took out two threats before they even got a shot off at my dad. Wyatt didn't earn his rank by fucking Forsaken's princess. He earned it through hard work, bloodshed, and loyalty. I had absolutely nothing to do with what he's accomplished.

Just a few seconds pass, though it feels like it's been several minutes. Wyatt's mouth is at my ear. He speaks so quietly that I have to strain to make sense of his mumbling. "Black van, far right. It's blocking the light post."

It's only now that I remember the 160-degree security mirror the club had installed on the light post for the guard on duty to see what's on the other side of the fence as he opens it. Except that right now the van is blocking the mirror, and the prospect is way too focused on what we're doing to pay attention to what's on the other side.

Wyatt walks around me to the prospect. He's got a hand up, ordering me to stay put. They exchange a few words with the prospect confirming that he's been keeping an eye on the van and has inspected the other side of the fence and that nobody's there. Wyatt claps him on the back, pulls out the piece he keeps tucked into the back waistband of his jeans, unlocks the safety, and then puts it back in place, covering it with his cut. Then he walks past the open gate toward the van.

I don't like it. It feels like a trap.

"Hey, Rink," I say and head over to him. He's still got the AR-15 in hand and is shielding himself from the street. If I'd been in doubt about the kind of fucked Forsaken is, the clubhouse gates being locked at all times and 24/7 prospect duty with heavy artillery sure as hell suffused my doubt. The threat from Mancuso is definitely greater than that of local law enforcement, I guess.

"I need your piece," I say and point to the waistband of his black jeans. He wrinkles a brow and shakes his head.

"No, ma'am," he says nervously.

"Either give me your personal gun, or I'll be taking this beauty right here," I say and place my hand on the barrel of the AR-15. "You play sniper or backup. Your choice."

"I'm not giving you my choppa," Rink says and hands over his .22.

I flick off the safety and give the kid a taunting smirk. I like him, so I won't tell the brothers about this, but I will tease him about it. Patting him on the shoulder, I say, "Oh, sweet boy, I'm from Detroit. That's only an AR-15. An AK-47 is a choppa."

I leave Rink there without looking back. He's on guard duty, which means Wyatt trusts him. So I trust him, too. I keep the gun down by my side, as hidden against my black yoga pants as possible. Wyatt is already storming up to the van, telling the dude in the driver's seat that he can't park there. The guy rolls down the passenger window and nods at Wyatt, promising to move. He talks quickly and stumbles over his words as he asks Wyatt how to get back to the highway. I watch from the distance, keeping both my man and this random dude in my sight. The driver gets out of the van, his door squeaking loudly upon his exit, and he walks around to Wyatt with the map in hand. For the briefest moment, I feel like my instincts have led me down a path of paranoia. This is insane. The dude is just lost.

A few cars pass by on Main Street, which happens to be what the highway turns into once you hit the town limits. Just as I'm relaxing and about to put the safety back on, the back door of the van slowly opens. It's soundless, really. If I weren't watching it happen, I wouldn't have any idea. The van itself is beat up, old, and not in the best repair. The driver's door squeaked when it was opened, but this one doesn't, which means one thing—I was right. This looks like a fucking hit on Forsaken, and oh hell to the fuck no is this going down.

Fear shoots through me. They couldn't know it would be Wyatt who would come out here to deal with the suspect vehicle. For a split second I hate that it's Wyatt. Even knowing that Rink and I have his back, having my man in danger never sits well with me. Zander hasn't even gotten his dad yet, and now this? Not on my watch.

A bruised and bloody man half stumbles out of the back of the van. He's holding one arm protectively against his chest. It looks broken. He has a knife in his other hand. He drags his feet on the pavement as he moves toward Wyatt. The noise catches Wyatt's attention, and he steps back from the bloodied man and the driver, his back now to me, as he draws his gun. The driver nods resolutely, and it's only now that I notice he's wearing a black suit. His olive complexion and the suit give him away immediately—Italian mafia.

"Mr. Segreti respectfully demands that our debt to Forsaken has been paid with the delivery of

Mr. Florentine, the man who put the wheels of our little spat in motion," the man in the suit says. Segreti? What the actual fuck has the club gotten themselves into? Their war was with Mancuso…

The man with the knife, now known as Mr. Florentine, lunges at Wyatt. Wy dodges him easily and screams at the man to put the knife down. Rink shouts from behind the fence, letting Wyatt know he's got his back. Florentine doesn't drop the knife. Instead, he lunges again, and this time, Wyatt puts his gun away and takes the fucker to the pavement.

Taking my eyes off Wyatt, I refocus my energy on the nameless driver. He scurries around the van to the driver's side. He's trying to get away, but he's not going to get far. I push off the concrete under my feet and run at the guy with Rink's gun in front of me. The man is half into the driver's seat by the time I reach him. He's got one hand in his suit jacket and the other on the steering wheel.

"By the time you pull your piece, the van will have a new paint job," I say evenly. He doesn't move, so to make him take me seriously, I close in and press the barrel of the .22 against the back of his skull and wait. Slowly, he removes his hands from his jacket and the steering wheel, putting them both in the air. Now that he's less of a threat, I remove my finger from the trigger and slam the butt of the gun into his head as hard as I can. He falls to the ground just a second later. He's face up, with his eyes closed and his mouth open. I back up and wait for the boys. I can hear them in the distance, all heavy feet and deep voices, as they rush out. Knowing they're on their way, I put the safety back on the gun and drop it to the ground.

"Amber!" Wyatt shouts as he rounds the van and grabs me from behind. I melt into him and close my eyes. He spins me around so my face is in his chest and lifts me up. I don't fight it. I just hold on to his neck and keep my face pressed into the base of his throat. I can be strong and tough. I can handle my shit—like I did with Rig—but that doesn't mean it doesn't keep me up at night. It doesn't mean I don't think about Rig's face right before he died as I kiss my boy good night and rock my baby girl to sleep. It doesn't mean I'm not haunted by it. It just means that I do what I was raised to—I protect my family even if it screws me up in the process. And I don't complain. I don't cry. I don't talk about it. Except for here, in Wyatt's arms, where I can be scared. Where, if even just for a moment, I can feel a little human and a little afraid.

CHAPTER TEN

I left the clubhouse as soon as I could. I don't run from a fight, never have. But it's different now. I'd never killed a man before either. But then my boy was taken right out from under me, and it was like a lifetime worth of guilt and doubt came crashing into me. Was I doing my best with my kids? Was I screwing them up more because I raised them, mostly, the way I'd been raised? Being a club kid isn't easy. A lot of women think they can handle the lifestyle, and then they get pregnant and realize they can't. My mother was never that woman. If anything, I'd only ever known her as this fierce creature who protected her family—*all of them*—at all costs. I've always prided myself on being just like her. I can handle anything.

At least I thought I could.

That scene back at the clubhouse didn't make a lot of sense. It's clear the boys are in more trouble out here than I thought, which only spurs another set of fears in me about the safety of my kids. What bothers me most is how I reacted to it. I hate feeling so vulnerable. That is by far the worst part of having kids. Your soft spot is obvious to every fucking asshole on the planet. Nobody has to touch me to hurt me—they just have to be a threat to my children, and suddenly my worst fears are coming true.

"Mom, I can't really breathe." Zander's voice is muffled by my shoulder blade. The moment I got back to my dad's house, I plopped down on the couch next to him and pulled him to me. I haven't let go since.

Dad's asked if I'm okay, to which I managed a terrible lie that promised him I'm fine. Piper abandoned her blocks on the floor in favor of crawling into my lap. Her presence made me feel a little better, but the truth is, I'm coming unhinged. This Segreti is a threat to my man and, by proxy, my children. Growing up in such a violent world makes you numb to the reality of it, I think. I'm not numb anymore.

"Sorry, baby," I say and pull back. Zander's eyes search mine for an answer. He knows something up. My boy's not stupid.

"What's going on?"

Honesty, Amber. You've always been honest with the kid.

"Your dad wants to see you," I say with a smile. The kid's entire fucking face lights up. He tries to play it cool, but I can see the hope in his eyes. "There was a scuffle at the club, but it's all good."

"You're lying," he says stiffly. My kid's got a bullshit detector most men would envy. Admittedly, he got that from his momma.

"Not about your dad, just about the club shit. Not our business, though."

"Since when has club business been none of yours?"

"Since I'm talking to my fourteen-year-old," I say. Zander knows basically nothing about the club's beef with Mancuso, and he definitely knows nothing about Segreti and whatever the hell is going on there, and I would just as soon it stays that way. I won't lie to him if he asks a direct question, but I do omit as much as I can.

"I won't be fourteen forever, lady." Zander huffs and pushes off from the couch. His voice has taken on a real grouchy tone that I don't much care for but can't do much about. Not unless I want to spend the whole of my waking hours dealing with it. My boy is already six feet—not surprising since his dad's six-foot-six—and something to contend with when I'm trying to ground his gargantuan ass. And right now, with the way his shoulders are heaving and his nostrils flaring, I can tell that he's fixing to earn himself some trouble. "I'm gonna have my cut one day, and I'll be the one who knows shit and doesn't tell you about it."

I take a deep breath as Piper stands and starts jumping up and down on my lap. She balances herself by grabbing at my nose and ear. It hurts like hell, but I try to focus on her brother. I narrow my eyes at Z and give him a devious smile. I'm way better at this game than he is.

"You'll need the president's approval. And do you really think he'll sign off on you prospecting if his old lady shuts that shit down?"

"That's just cold, Mom," he says and kicks at the carpet.

In the distance, I can hear a Harley approaching. My eyes fall closed for half a second. I instinctively know who it is. Piper pulls at my nose, shooting throbbing pain through my head and face. Shit. I gently take her little hand and pretend to eat it.

"Take your sister to your room." I wipe my face free of baby drool and hand Piper to her brother. Zander expertly takes her with one arm and walks away without argument. I have to work to wipe the shock from my face. Zander normally argues about everything, so to say I'm suspect would be an understatement. I don't have time for that, though.

My feet carry me across the room quickly as I rush to the front door and peer out. Dad's house is a little ramshackle ranch on a couple of acres just outside Fort Bragg. His closest neighbors are far enough away that I've never actually met them and don't even know what they look like. I doubt he does either. Even if I didn't know the sound of Wyatt's Harley, I'd know it was Forsaken approaching. Nobody else comes out here—especially not on a bike.

With a steely resolve, I walk out of the house and shut the door firmly behind me. The house is shielded by tall redwoods that blanket the surrounding land in a shadow that the sun rarely breaks through. Through the dotted landscape, I can just make out the shiny chrome on its approach. The closer it gets, the better I can see the rider. Wyatt's massive frame straddles his Harley. He rides through the last few trees that were hiding his approach and comes fully into view. His tall, hulking frame is perched on a shiny black bike with sparkling chrome pipes that growl as he flies down the dirt road.

His hair is longer than it's ever been, down past his shoulders now. It blows in the wind, slapping at his cheeks and getting caught on the black sunglasses he wears beneath his half helmet. My stomach knots. Suddenly I feel like I did back in Michigan when I was sixteen and waiting for Wyatt to pick me up. Mishy and I lived in this house with Dad when we came out here, but I was only here for a few weeks before I officially moved in with Wyatt.

Dad's napping right now, probably sleeping off a fifth of tequila, but he's heard the bike no doubt. At least, that's how my luck's gone lately. I just hope he stays inside if he's conscious. As far as I know, he and Wyatt haven't seen each other in years, and for now at least, I'd like to keep it that way. The green plastic sandbox in the shape of a turtle that Dad bought Piper catches my attention, reminding me that there's more important things to talk to Wyatt about than his and Dad's beef.

He pulls up, cuts the engine, props her up, and pulls off his helmet. A ball forms in my throat as I watch him move. He's been riding since he was fifteen—much to #mom# chagrin—and it shows. He handles the large Harley as if it weighs nothing. The taut muscles in his arms are on full display in the black wifebeater he wears under his cut, showing off the tattoos that cover most of his flesh. I mentally note that he's changed from what he was wearing earlier—well, his shirt at least.

"Ran out on me," he says. His voice makes it sound like he's thirsty, so gravely and rough. "Last time I remember you running out on me, you were eight months pregnant with our fuckin' son. Don't like seeing you leave me."

"We need to talk," I say quickly before he can reach me.

"You need to quit fucking leaving me."

"Quit giving me reason to!" That's not totally fair. It's not exactly his fault the Italian guys showed up when they did. It's not one hundred percent his fault that Rig targeted Zander. But it doesn't exactly matter either. Ever since Rig, I've been on edge and my moods are fluctuating like crazy. I don't like these feelings. Adding Wyatt to the mix turns my crazy into straight-up insanity.

Wyatt storms toward me, grabs me around the waist and pulls me against him. He tips my face up toward his. And all his gentle turns into something else entirely in the blink of an eye.

"Knock it the fuck off!" He screams in my face, so loud, but I barely hear the words.

The ball in my throat hardens, and I'm forced to swallow it. My hands shake with an anger that I don't expect. I don't know why I'm so mad right now, but I am. Nervous, sure. Anxious, yeah. But mad? That one confuses me. I don't dwell on it, though, because the frustration becomes too much to swallow. I push him off me, angry and annoyed. I suck in an unsteady breath as we stare each other down. He huffs. My eyes fall to his lips and stay there. It's magnetic, the pull his lips have over me. Every time I look at them, I'm either desperate to touch them, or I remember every vile word he's ever said to me. If I'm being honest with myself, even then, in those moments of remembrance, I still want his mouth on me. Nothing ever changes that. I hate admitting that, even to myself, though.

I pull my gaze from his lips to find his eyes are on my mouth. His tongue pokes out, drags over his rough lips. I could fall into this. I could let this happen so easily, but then we'll end up right back where we started.

"You can't kiss me. You're going to hate me soon, so please don't kiss me."

"What?" His mood has shifted. A sly smile breaks out on his face. He's gorgeous when he smiles. His hands hold me in place tighter than before but still gentle. I missed this so much. Wyatt's the only man I've ever known who can be so rough and demanding while still touching me like I'm something precious. As much as I've missed his touch, I'm going to miss it even more when he hates me.

"You're going to hate me," I say again, only this time louder. My heart breaks at the thought of pushing him away, but I do it anyway. I shove him off me and scrub my face with my hands. "You're not going to want me when you know what I've done."

My voice is raised, as if he won't hear me unless I'm screaming. I have to get this out, though, and if it comes out as a shout, oh well. But it doesn't seem to matter how loud I say it, because he just stares at me in bewilderment.

"I don't know why you're acting like this, but I'm fucking over it. My woman knows what she wants, and she goes after it. She doesn't act like some scared little fucking girl, so knock it off. You keep this shit up, and you're right, I might not want you."

He's not getting it. I need him good and mad so he can leave. If he stays here, he's just going to get Zander and Dad's attention, and I really don't want that. What he said earlier—about me being different—I am. So much has happened since that month we conceived Piper. So much is different now. *I'm* different.

And I need him to understand, so I tell him the one thing I don't want to. The one thing that makes me feel like shit.

"I was sleeping with Rig." I hate the way it sounds coming out of my mouth. Nothing about that admission or the fact that it happened makes me feel anything close to okay. Letting Rig take my body is a huge betrayal to Wyatt. Huge in the way that might be worse than not telling him about Piper. I won't tell him how it started, I can't. Not even if it spares me his wrath. I'm not that girl.

I'm not.

Half a second after I say it, he explodes. An angry, distraught scream bellows from him. Not even in the form of words, but just pain with a side of hatred. His face screws up, with squinted eyes and a nasty snarl on his lips. I need to explain, to clarify that Rig didn't make his move until a few years after Zander was born.

"You always wanted to fuck him, didn't you?"

My eyes fall closed. I can't even look at the disgust in his eyes anymore. From the looks of it, I sure led with the worse of two evils. I knew Wyatt would be angry, and I shouldn't be surprised at the hurt on his face. Somehow, though, I am. My head feels stuffy, swollen, and it's only now that I realize I've stopped breathing. I suck in a deep, shaky breath to balance myself out. I need to get a grip, or I'll never get through this.

"When?"

I don't catch the question until Wyatt has to repeat himself. This is different. He's never been one for asking many questions.

"Not until Zander was three." I force myself to open my eyes and meet his. I feel like this confession should somehow diffuse his anger, but it doesn't. His grip on my face gets harder, so hard that it starts to hurt. I lock my jaw, forcing myself to deal with it. Old ladies don't cry, and we sure as fuck don't whine about stupid shit. I always try to represent my man, even when we're not together, even when we haven't seen each other in years. Even after this, I'll still be Wyatt's. Even though he won't want me and he won't be mine, I'll never not belong to him. That's what being voted in means, and for the millionth time since I ran from him, I'm grateful for it. I can't imagine not being tied to Wyatt in some way.

"You stupid whore." The words tumble out of his mouth with such raw pain that I can't feel anything but sorrow. "We were together after that. You told me you'd never touched him."

I lied.

"It's not—" I start but clamp up immediately. The words hang there, on the cliff of a confession that I refuse to make. I stare up at my man, watching his eyes glass over and his breathing slow. He doesn't look so much angry now as he does hurt. I don't expect this new Wyatt, don't really know what to make of him. The old Wyatt would have flown off the handle and called it a day. He wouldn't be standing here. He wouldn't be trying. The realization that he has changed, at least in a few important ways, sends a ripple of emotion flying through me. I blink back the tears.

Wyatt opens his mouth to speak, but a loud noise startles him. He turns his face toward the house and freezes for a long moment. Then his hands drop to his sides, and he just stands there, the steel in his body disappears. I try to pull my eyes away from him, but I can't. My man looks like he just found Jesus on toast or something miraculous like that. As big and tough as he is, in this moment he looks so vulnerable and broken.

"Don't yell at my mom." The too-deep-for-his-age angry voice of my son shouts from behind me. My stomach falls to my feet as my head whips around. I've been waiting for this moment for years. Zander's been waiting his entire life. Fourteen years of hope and dreams and want have all been wrapped up in this moment. And now it's happening, and he's being his bossy teenage self. I don't know if I want to laugh or cry. I never wanted Zander to meet his father like this—in the middle of a fight.

Wyatt takes a few steps toward the house, his eyes glued to Zander. His voice is faint but clear when he whispers, "My boy."

He moves so quickly that before I know it, he's rushed at Zander and has thrown his arms around our son. I'm left standing in the dirt, staring at the two of them, doing the best I can to hold back the tears. It's useless. If my mom were here right now, I like to think she'd forgive me this weakness. All I can see from here are Zander's gangly arms as they wrap around his dad for the first time in his entire life. Fuck. I can't believe I let anything, even Wyatt's addiction, keep them apart.

Just when I don't think I could feel any lower, a high-pitched baby scream comes from inside the house.

Piper.

Crap.

Now is so not the time for her to make her grand entrance with her dad. I've already been here too long to have not told him about her, but the situation with Zander has really complicated things. Wyatt's known about Zander—he's already dealt with the blow from finding out that my boy is, for sure, his. Maybe it's selfish, but I want my guys to have their time before I throw my toddler into the mix. I don't get that luxury, though, because Zander pulls back from his dad and rushes toward the house. I chase after him, hoping like hell that my baby girl isn't hurt. Zander flings the door open, when I'm just a few steps behind him. I can feel Wyatt standing right behind me, his blissed-out expression slides right back into that desperate sorrow he was sporting earlier.

Kids.

He probably thinks Piper isn't his. Especially after that confession about Rig. No wonder he looks so upset. Standing there in the front doorway is the bombshell I had yet to drop. She's so cute and small. Not small for her age, mind you. No, she's tall, just like her dad and brother, but still tiny in comparison. Her red face is streaked with tears, and she has a stuffed dog squished to her chest.

CHAPTER ELEVEN

Wyatt—

My boy.

Zander Wyatt Strand stands in front of the house now. Fuck. It feels damn good to touch him, to know he's real. He's taller than I expect—already several inches taller than Amber. He got broad shoulders, a square jaw, and a long, straight nose. He's kind of gangly, not having yet gained his muscle mass. Looking at my boy is like looking at an old photograph of myself. A flash of anger courses through me at the idea of Amber spending every day looking at him, talking with him, and never reaching out to me. I have to remind myself of how fucked up I was back then. If I'm being honest with myself, I didn't really get a handle on my shit until recently. I know she tried. She did. It doesn't stop the irrational jealousy that courses through me at all the time she's had with our boy that I've missed out on. Just about six months before we headed out to Brooklyn, I got clean once and for all.

Without even realizing what I'm doing, I head for Zander and wrap him in a tight hug. My brothers wouldn't begrudge me this, but fuck if I'm not glad they're nowhere around right now. It takes him a moment before my boy lifts his arms and hugs me back. And fuck if it's not the best. His grip isn't as tight on me as mine is on him, but that's okay. I'm just a dude to him. He must know who I am, but it's still not the same. I don't know if I got that until now, but I do. The love I feel for my mom isn't really less, but it's certainly not the same as what I feel for my boy. If I feel this strongly about him now, I can only imagine how Amber must feel. Or how Grady feels about Chey. He's had eighteen years of that kid, and I know damn well how protective he is. Now that she's off at school in the city, he stalks around in a mood if he hasn't seen her in a while. It's like no matter how much time he's had with her, it's never enough. I envy him that—those years with her that I didn't get with my boy.

It's my fault.

Sucking in a deep, cathartic breath, I let my eyes fall closed and savor the moment. Fourteen years that I've squandered on shit that brought me nothing but trouble and grief. Just when I'm letting myself feel all kinds of self-pity and shit, a loud, high-pitched scream comes from inside the house. It sounds like a small child. Zander stiffens in my arms and pull away. I let him go and brace myself for it—that moment when my fears become reality.

Amber has kids—as in plural—not just the one we have together. I try like hell, but fail miserably, at keeping my emotions in check. Amber Wallace—my woman, my fucking old lady—slept with Rig. I've hated that guy for so damn long that I didn't realize I could possibly hate him more than I did the night he suggested he'd been fucking my pregnant old lady. But then she laid that bomb on me, like I'm supposed to just flip a goddamn switch and hate her or something.

If it weren't for Zander coming out when he did, busting my balls for yelling at his mom, I might be halfway there. I could never hit her, but fuck if I didn't want to hit something and see blood. So many questions swirled in my mind, like wanting to know exactly when it started between them. Wanting to know how and why. It's the whys that will keep me up at night, I think. After everything Rig did to us back then, why would she let him into her bed? I'm spiraling and I know it, but I don't have the power to stop myself. Zander pulled me out of it once, but this time, I don't think even my boy can stop me from completely imploding.

Amber has at least one more kid with someone else. She wanted, more than anything, to make me leave right before Zander came out. Telling me about Rig was only important if…I can't bring myself to say it, but the thoughts are flying through my brain at a mile a minute. Rig fucked my old lady, planted his fucking kid in her belly, and probably played daddy to my son, too. If I weren't such a pussy, I'd probably take my own piece to my ear and call it a goddamn day. I did this. I let this happen. I let that fucker into her life and then left her with him. I left my boy to deal with him, and it's my fault that when Rig's back was against the wall, he took my boy. I made that choice when I chose all that bullshit over my woman. I made her a killer, and that, above everything else, is what I won't ever be able to forgive myself for.

I snap back to the present when Zander and Amber rush toward the noise. The door swings open and blows my entire world apart. Standing in the doorway is the most pissed-off-looking tiny human I think I've ever seen. He's got a stuffed dog clutched to his chest. Chubby little fingers dig into the dog's neck as he holds it protectively. I eye his face to try to figure out what I'm looking at, but all I see is angry kid. His face is wet with tears, his bottom lip is jutted out, and he's glaring at his big brother. With the most defiant little expression, he says, "Bad!" Then he looks around, and his face falls on Amber and all of the anger slides right off of his face as he runs to her. She scoops him into her arms, and it's only now that I see it—the truth. His eyes are the same distinct blue-green color that looks similar to what I see every day in the mirror.

Amber turns to face me with red cheeks. She's flustered. The nervousness in her eyes is amplified, and she's hopping from foot to foot. She's jittery and her jaw ticks, a sure sign she's gearing up for a fight.

"How old is he?"

Her brow furrows and she purses her lips. "Almost two."

"Tell me, baby," I whisper. I stare into her eyes, desperate to tell her how badly I need to hear it. We were fucking like crazy a few years back, but if I let myself believe he's mine only to find out it's not true, I'm going to lose my shit. All this stuff with my boy and my old lady is heavy enough without adding this to the mix. I can't let myself want this kid to be mine until I know he really is. Amber still doesn't speak. My arm stretches out, and I glide my fingers over her cheek. She takes in a deep breath and releases it slowly.

And she nods. She fucking nods, and I swear to Christ there's a small smile playing at her lips. She's practically shaking with her silent omission. Her voice is strained and low when she speaks, and it hits me right in the gut. "I tried to call you. I wanted you to know, but you wouldn't take my call. So I just..."

My hand wraps itself around the back of her neck, and I pull her to me, placing a kiss on her forehead. I squeeze my eyes shut in an effort to stop myself from crying like a bitch. I'm careful not to get too close to her. I don't want to squish our boy.

When I pull away, I see Zander is standing beside us. His hands are shoved into his pockets, and he stares at my bike to his left. "Her name's Piper," he says.

Our little boy isn't a boy after all. She's a girl. A tiny little girl with a temper like her momma and blue-green eyes like her daddy. She's fucking perfect.

"She's wearing blue," I say in defense. I thought parents color-coded their kids and shit. I feel like an asshole. What kind of father doesn't know his own child? What kind of dad doesn't know he has a daughter?

The kind that's a fuckup.

"Are you mad?" The question comes from Zander. It takes me aback. I stare at him for a long moment before

I realize that this is a part of parenting I've missed out on. Answering those kinds of questions that you don't know how. I've seen it with Grady through the years, wondering if I'd make the same choices he has. I always come out realizing that I don't know what the fuck I'd do. Because back then, fantasizing about having Baby Z and Mugs back in my life was just that—a fucking fantasy. The only thing I had was the what-ifs.

"No," I say. It's too complicated to explain to a kid.

Amber shuffles and clears her throat, saying, "I don't lie to him. Tell him the truth."

"It is the truth." I stare her down for a long minute before stepping away and walking to my boy. For being so tall and with such broad shoulders, right now he looks so much younger than his fourteen years. I don't know how I'm going to explain the situation to him, or if he'd even understand, but I can't fuck Amber over with this. She tells me to be honest with him, so I'll do it and hope for the best.

Fuck, I hate this shit.

"Hey," I say to get his attention, but he doesn't look at me. Irritation swells in me, but I fight hard to bite it back. "Dude, come on." The change in tone from father to club president gets his attention. His eyes are watery and a little red in the center. Fuck. No wonder he didn't want to look at me.

"I'm pissed," I say. He stares at me with shock all over his face. Shit. He looks so much like I did when I was his age. "Because I fucked up. No kid should grow up without their dad. I'm pissed because I was a goddamn idiot and should have fought for you and your mom. I was into a lot of bad shit until recently, and it cost me my son. That fucking hurts. Finding out I got a little girl—a baby I fucking begged your mom for—that tears me up. But I'm not pissed at her. That shit's on me. You don't take a woman like your mom and fuck her over. Not ever."

Zander stands so still, eyeing me warily. He probably only heard about half of what I said, if even. But Amber heard, and that's enough for now.

"Are you going to leave?"

Fuck. I just want to hug the kid and not let go of him. I used to think about what he'd be like when he was born, or if he'd be into sports or cars like I was. I spent so much time wondering what my boy would be like, but not any of those dreams, no matter how big or grand, live up to even a fraction of the reality of having this kid stand in front of me and asking me a question like that. This is the reason I got clean—so I could have and remember moments like this. I just didn't know I'd ever get them.

"Nope. Never. I'm going to be so far up your ass, you're going to think I'm toilet paper."

Zander laughs like I'm joking, but he's got a goofy smile on his face, and fuck if it isn't the best thing I've seen all day.

"Good," Amber says from behind me. "It's almost dinnertime."

CHAPTER TWELVE

In this moment, everything is perfect. My family—my old lady and my beautiful, perfect kids—are sitting around Thumper's old wooden kitchen table. I'm leaning back in my chair, just chilling as I watch the three of them interact. Amber pulls me into conversation every now and then, and Zander is quiet as hell, but he keeps staring at me like I've got two heads or something. I want to talk to him, but when I try, I just fucking freeze up and can't. Piper is in her high chair and talking her little baby ass off in a language that Amber pretends to speak, but she can't possibly. Her conversational skills are about as solid as mine are when I'm fucked-up—nothing makes any sense.

Amber's eyes shift to mine and she tries—and fails—to subtlety nod her head in Zander's direction. My eyes widen and I shrug my shoulders. The woman's got to give me some help here. I don't know how to be a dad. Fuck.

"Do you like movies?" I ask Zander. His eyes shoot to mine immediately, but he doesn't speak. He just nods his head. I suck in an unsteady breath and stand.

"Are you leaving?" His face pales, and his eyes bounce from me to his mom. His brows draw together, and his knuckles are white as he grips his fork like his life depends on it.

"Just getting another beer," I say and give him my best smile. I probably look like a serial killer or something. Fuck. This is probably easier when they're babies and don't know how awkward and weird their parents are. I just want the kid to like me.

Amber signals she wants a beer, so I head out to the garage and grab two cold ones from the fridge. Once I have them in my hands, I give myself a minute before heading back in there. I'm not this uncertain fuck who gets nervous around people who can't kill me before I can kill them. But this is different. Zander isn't a prospect—he's my son. I can't force him to respect me, and he's not going to kiss my ass and pretend he likes me. My cut won't buy me shit with my kid, and it's fucking me up thinking that who I am underneath the patch isn't enough to be a good dad for whatever time I have before he's too grown to want me around.

Back in the kitchen, Amber is leaning across the table, saying something to Zander that I can barely hear. I move closer but not too close to be seen. My boy keeps a stiff upper lip as she talks, offering only an occasional verbal response.

"It's okay to be excited," she says.

He rolls his eyes and says, "I'm not excited. He's cool is all."

Amber shakes her head and focuses on Piper, who's trying to grab macaroni and cheese in her little hand and shove it in her mouth, but they keep slipping out, and she's getting mad. My girl's got a temper, just like her momma.

"Fork works better," Zander says, eyeing his sister. She's stares at him, then picks up her plastic fork and waves it at him. Her lips are pursed, parted slightly, and she's doing this spitting/shushing thing and giving him a warning look.

"Bubba, be nice!" she says in a little baby shout. A stupid fucking smile and laugh overtake me. She must have practiced that a lot because it comes out so clear compared to everything else she tries to say. Striding into the room, I'm met with a perplexed look from Zander and a soft smile from Amber.

"She's bossy," I say and pop the top off Amber's beer before handing it to her.

"She's a pain in the ass," Zander says, giving her a side eye. My smile gets bigger as I open my own beer and sit back down in my seat.

"You both get that from your mother," I say. Amber told me bits and pieces about my boy, and one recurring theme was how strong-headed he is. Something shifts in his mood. He drops his fork, shoves his chair back, and stands up so quickly it surprises me. What the actual fuck?

"Sit your ass down and finish your dinner." Amber's order does nothing to derail the boy from the attitude he's cooking.

"No. He can't just come in here and act like he knows me!"

A lump forms in my throat. He's right. I did just meet him, and hearing the pain and emotion in his voice takes me back to being his age and being pissed at the world for anything and everything. But most especially at the time, for not having a dad. I let my boy grow without a dad, and damn if this doesn't suck.

"Sit down." Amber's voice has taken on a hard edge that demands a sudden response. But he still doesn't move. If it wouldn't make the situation worse, I'd point out that this kind of shit is exactly what I was referring to. Amber goes about trying to talk to the boy, but every second that passes, my mood just gets worse and worse.

"Why? So we can sit here and pretend like we're a happy fucking family?"

Amber shoots up from her chair before I can. She crosses the room and stands right in front of him. I can tell they've done this dance at least a hundred times before. I rise from my seat slowly, taking in greedy breaths to calm myself. It. Doesn't. Fucking. Help.

"Zander Wyatt Strand, you get your fucking ass *back* in that goddamn chair. *Now.*" Amber's voice is harder than I've ever heard it before. Half a second later, Piper is screaming at the top of her lungs. Her face is bright red, with tears streaming down her chubby cheeks. Her little arms are shaking like crazy.

Zander leans down and shakes his head with a cocky smirk on his face. "No."

I will not beat his ass.

"Kid, you're one wrong word from getting your ass whooped." Amber jabs her finger into his chest and stands on tiptoe to get in his face as much as she can. I want to do something, but I don't think knocking my kid out the first time I meet him is going to go over well with him or his mother. And that's kind of all I got in terms of ideas right now, so I stay put and do my best not to fuck him up.

"Which word?" he says. "*Bite* or *me*?"

I will not beat my son's ass.

"How many times have you begged me to let you see your dad, huh? And this is how you act? You're hurting, kid. I get that. But you need to rein it in and fucking enjoy having a father."

My woman is in crazy momma bear mode right now—laying down the law while appealing to his heart. Her chest is heaving and her movements are jerky, but her voice is clear as day. Too bad Zander's skull is too fucking thick for him to hear a damn thing she's saying. He's cocky, throwing his size around like he's the biggest motherfucker in the room. *He's not.*

The kid is at least half a foot taller than her, and though he's lacking muscle, he's hearty. Shit. If he were a brother and she were some random bitch, she'd have her ass handed to her right now for giving him shit. Not that Mugs couldn't handle herself in that situation, but it's crazy to see the difference in size. She's small compared to me—most people are—but seeing how our son towers her is just one more reminder of how much of his life I've missed. I'll never see him shorter than her. I'll never see any of that.

All I have left is the smart-mouth teenager who's smirking at his mother like he ain't got a thing to lose.

He ignores her and walks right past his mom, meeting my eye for the briefest moment before the smirk falls from his face. My expression remains impassive as I watch him totally ignore her when he says, "Going out."

"You are not leaving this house," she turns and yells. Her exhausted eyes fall on mine. She mouths, "*Help*," before turning and picking up Piper and holding her to her chest.

Well then. It looks like I have to figure out how to parent right now after all. So, I follow him out the front door and onto the lawn. He stops about ten feet from the house and looks around at the mass of grass and trees that surround us. He can stalk off, but there's nowhere to go. He turns his head toward me just slightly before continuing on his path.

"Z!" I don't follow, hoping that my voice will carry enough to bring him home. It doesn't. "Stop." I make sure my tone is as no-nonsense and hard-as-nails as I can get it. It's the tone I reserve for Church when the boys can't shut up but they need to, or when something goes wrong and somebody is about to die for their mistakes. I obviously can't deal with Zander the way I want to when he's like this. The boy doesn't want a father right now, so instead he's getting the club president.

"I have to come to you, your punishment is going to be far worse than if you come back to me."

He stands fifteen feet away, torn between doing what he wants and what I've told him to do.

"That's one," I say, taking a step toward him. "Every step I have to take toward you is a week of shit you do *not* want to have to deal with. And believe me, boy, the closer I have to move to get to you, the angrier I'm going to be when I get there."

It's a long moment before he turns around, but he fucking does. His face is red, his shoulder hunched, and his jaw is set. He takes one step toward me and stops. "How many steps will it take for you to leave again?"

I swear to fucking Christ, I will not beat this little fucker's ass.

"That ain't happening," I say. My temper still flares, but I recognize what he's doing. It's the same thing I did to my mom when I first met her about thirty years ago. Still, it's taking everything in me not to totally snap on the boy. "I'm here. I'm not leaving."

"Bullshit."

Nope.

Going to beat his ass.

"Boy, I do not have the patience or the practice to put up with your shit. Get your ass over here before I show you how I'd deal with this kind of disrespect from a fucking prospect."

He watches me carefully as he takes a single step forward, then folds his arms over his chest and stops.

I take another step forward, saying, "And that's two."

"Please," he says with a hard jerk of his chin, "A two-week stretch is nothing."

Another step. "Three."

He steps toward me again, and now we're just a few feet away. I swing my right arm out and hook it behind his neck. He pulls back quickly to dodge me, but it doesn't work. Pulling him into me, I hug the little fucker so hard that I'm not sure he can breathe. This is the only thing I know how to do. It's what my mom did when I thought she'd leave me and I acted out so bad to make sure I didn't love another person who didn't want me.

"What are you doing?" He manages to speak despite his face being shoved into my cut. His lanky body squirms to get away, but he's no match for the twenty-two years and hundred pounds I've got on him.

"Showing you that I'm not going to leave you," I say and hold him tighter. My muscles ache for a reprieve after a few minutes. My back starts to ache not long after that. I feel the need to yawn as the sun sets around us, but still, I don't let go. I just hold on and wait. Because eventually he'll relax into me. And when he does, I let out a deep breath but don't loosen my grip on him. His chin wobbles against my chest and his body shakes, though ever so slightly. I can feel it. I know what he's doing, and I won't shame him or worry him by letting go and acknowledging it.

Eventually, long after the sun has set, he whispers into my chest, "You're really not leaving?"

And my heart breaks, because no, I'm not.

I'm not ever leaving.

CHAPTER THIRTEEN

Amber

Piper's eyelids slowly fall closed. It's just a moment, a single blissful moment, before they pop open again and she's staring up at me like I'm about to perform a magic act. I don't normally hold her as she falls asleep anymore, but I am tonight.

It's been a big day for our little family. While Piper may be too young to understand who Wyatt is, she understands all the drama around her. She knows something is wrong when her brother is yelling and I'm yelling back. She hates it. As it is, she wasn't sleeping well when her brother wasn't home because Rig had kidnapped him. Now she's very slowly adjusting to our new, albeit temporary, space. For tonight, she's just not up for falling asleep on her own in her Pack 'n Play. At least not with the big scary biker staring at her. I don't know if she's actually afraid of him, or if she's just curious. He looks at her the way he used to look at me. Like he's looking at his entire world. It's similar to the way he looks at Zander, but not quite.

She lifts her little head and turns to look at Wyatt. I can't really see her expression from this angle, but whatever face she's making is making him laugh. I smile. It's probably the first happy, genuine smile I've had in weeks. Since before we came out to California and uprooted our entire lives. Long before Rig dared take my boy. I don't know when last time was that I smiled like this, if I'm being truthful. But here I am, in my old bedroom, with my old man and our daughter. And she's making him smile, and that makes me smile. I'm not a religious person, and I've never been the praying type, but in this moment, I feel blessed.

"What is she doing?" I ask. They're having some kind of silent conversation that has Wyatt raising his eyebrows and making swoon-worthy faces at our daughter. No wonder I was a teen mom. The man's always wanted kids, takes family very seriously, and can pretty much force an ovary explosion any time he wants. *Asshole.*

"She's batting her eyes at me," Wyatt says through muffled laughter. His voice is so quiet, and his body is so close. We're just hanging out on my bed in my old bedroom like no time has passed at all. But it has. A lot of time has passed, and it kills me that I can't just enjoy this shit.

"The sassy little flirt is trying to get out of bedtime," I say. She learned to bat her eyes recently. I swear to Christ that I don't know who fucking taught her that shit, but she picked it up and has been using it go get her way ever since. Sometimes she looks like she's having a seizure, because she's still a baby and doesn't have perfect control over her movements just yet. Other times, it looks so practiced it worries me for her teenage years.

Wyatt leans in and tickles her chubby little neck. She squirms in my arms and giggles relentlessly before eventually subsiding into a frustrated yawn. Irritation spikes in me before I can stop it, and I lose my little bit of happy. I'm glad they're bonding, but he's riling her up, and that just pisses me off. It's hard enough to keep her on a routine without this shit.

Because as surely as Zander is going to mouth off at some point, Piper will wake up at the ass crack of dawn. And that means she's going to be grouchy. She's going to be grouchy and miserable tomorrow, and if I don't get her to bed soon, there's nothing I can do about it. But I can't deny either of them this moment. She deserves to bond with her dad, and he needs to learn how to be her dad. So I bite my tongue. No matter how much it bothers me, and no matter how much I'd rather not be the adult here, I stay silent and try to look happy.

She's giggling and reaching out for him, but when he moves closer, she puts up her little hand and says, "No." *No* is her favorite word. I should tell him that, so he doesn't take it personally. But I don't. Because now there's light in her eyes that tells me she won't go to sleep for at least another hour, and no matter how much I want to move out of this bed, she won't let me. The only thing worse than sitting here for another hour while I wait for her to calm down would be to stick her in her mobile crib. If I take away her new friend and subject her to the inhumane task of soothing herself to sleep, she won't let me hear the end of it. My girl is a fussy little thing, but thankfully she tires easily despite my fears. Obviously I'm a monster. After Piper *finally* falls into a soundless sleep, and when I know she won't wake, I move her to her travel crib.

Wyatt opens his mouth to speak as we're sneaking out of the room, but I place my finger over his lips. He raises an eyebrow and takes a step closer to me. He's charged. With his smoldering eyes, intense focus, and ragged breathing, he's the sexiest fucking thing I've ever seen. All testosterone and muscles and a defiant energy that just sucks me in. Oh hell, this is exactly how I got pregnant with both of our kids.

Now is not the time, and I'm really not in the mood. I was hoping to end this day without another fight, but it looks like it's heading that direction anyway. Wyatt wants us, I can tell. I shouldn't have touched him. Even if it was as innocent as keeping him quiet.

After Zander and Wyatt had their little blowout in the yard, Dad finally woke up and came out of his room. He marched right up to Wyatt and took a swing at him. Unfortunately, poor old dad is exactly that. Old. Once I hit thirty, I tried to limit the number of times I called anyone old, because I don't really like it when my son tells me I'm ancient. But Dad is, for all intents and purposes, old. His body is worn, he's a total curmudgeon, and he probably tells us every single day that he's "too old for this shit." It doesn't even matter what "this shit" is, or the fact that "this shit" changes on the hour, but he's too old and too tired of it. So when dad takes a swing at Wyatt, who has obviously kept up the weight lifting over the years, it doesn't end in his favor. Thankfully,

Zander was watching, and Wyatt went easy on his former president. Proof that even Neanderthals can check their egos once in a while.

"Don't look at me like that," I hiss once the bedroom door is closed.

Wyatt either chooses to ignore my mood or plays dumb, because he hooks his arm around my waist and pulls me against him. His chest is hard, the taut muscles in his arms are hard, and his breathing is getting even harder than it was before. I suck in a deep breath and am rewarded with a low groan. His hand travels from my lower back to my ass, and he presses me against him. Not surprisingly, his dick is hard, too. His other hand cups my chin and tilts my face up toward his. I could let this happen, and I would enjoy every moment of it. But I don't want to. I'm a mother now. I can't do this to Zander again.

"How am I looking at you? Am I looking at you like you just made my fucking dreams come true? Like watching you soothe our little girl to sleep is the best goddamn thing I've seen in my entire life? Like all I can think about when I see you with our kids is how I want to pound your pussy raw until we have another? That how you don't want me looking at you?"

My jaw shakes. My hands shake. Hell, my entire fucking body is alight from what he's said. He means every single word of it. But that doesn't mean he'll be able to stay clean and stick around long enough to see the baby he wants so badly be born.

So I take a deep breath and say, "Yeah. That's exactly how I don't want you looking at me."

I pull away and rush down the hallway as quietly as I can. I'm not about to wake up Piper, but I need some air. Zander passed out on the couch instead of in Mishy's old bedroom, so I'm mindful of him as I slip out the front door and walk through the grass until I get to the tree Wyatt carved our names into.

The trunk of the redwood is massive, as most of them are, but it's crooked in spots, like it sprouted up wrong or something. I lean against the trunk without trying to find the carving and just breathe. I calm myself as much as I can by closing my eyes and just enjoying the peace and quiet of the moment. It won't last, but I have it for this minute, and that's what matters. Just as I feel my body relax, the creak of the front door alerts me to the fact that I'm not alone.

When Wyatt's so close that I can physically feel his presence, I open my eyes. His arms are crossed over his chest. Both are huge—the muscles in his arms defined and his chest broad. I used to love his size. I'm sure I still do. It's just that right now I'm not feeling very loving toward him.

"You're fucking punishing me," he says.

I blow out a hostile breath and shake my head.

"What happened at the club today?"

"You know what happened. You were there."

That's not what I mean, and he knows it.

"I don't want you involved in club business. I want you and our kids as far away from that shit as possible."

"That's not possible, and you know it!" I'm seething. We both know how today went down. I didn't stick my nose in where it didn't belong. I was just there when everything spun out of control. He can't honestly expect that telling me to stay out of it is going to work or that it'll make everything better. As if he could fully separate his life with the club and his life with his kids. Idiot.

"I'm cleaning up the mess. That's all you need to know."

"You never used to leave me out." It's a truth he can't deny, even though I can tell he wants to—desperately—in this moment.

"You didn't used to be a mother." His words hang between us, taunting me. My face scrunches up in detest. *How dare he.* The only thing I can do is glare at him, but it does nothing to work him up. His eyes are trained on mine, and he's so earnest it pisses me off.

"I'm a mother—to *your* kids, might I add—but I'm also your old lady. I didn't just stop being a woman when I had kids, so don't you *dare* treat me like I'm fragile and can't handle my shit."

"That's not what I meant!" He's shouting now.

"Tell me what's going on. You know as well as I do that keeping shit from your old lady is dangerous. I can't help you or the club if you keep me in the dark."

Something I've said makes his jaw lock in place, his hands ball into fists at his sides, and his eyes turn dark. He's getting angry, which is about the only thing that will get me what I want.

"Are you my old lady? Doesn't seem like it—you won't even let me fucking touch you."

I flinch. I'm not that woman who mouths off and can't take it when shit's thrown back at her, but this hurts. It hurts because I want to let him touch me. I want to touch him. I want to fall back into that crazy, passionate couple we used to be. I want to walk into a room by his side and have every single goddamn person there know we're a packaged deal. He is mine and I am his, and there isn't a single thing on this earth that can change that. But he's right. That girl who walked into a room, knowing she owns her man, wasn't a mother. She didn't have two kids who depend on her to make the best choices for them. Her old man was her entire world, but now he's not. He can't be. Not until my kids are adults and their worlds won't fucking end because Daddy's on a bender. I need to keep things straight with us, calm even, so that I can make sure he stays sober.

Wyatt takes a step closer and cages me in with an arm on each side of me. A slow, devious smile breaks out on his face, and he's got a flicker in his eyes that tells me he's gearing up to be a real asshole. He used to get his way by out-bitching me, but that was before I went pro by having a teenager. I steel myself for the verbal assault I just know is coming.

"You are fucking punishing me, and it's going to stop. I fucked up, okay? I snorted shit, popped pills, lost time, lost you, our son, and everything else that fucking matters to me except for my cut. But let's get this straight—I'm clean. Have been since I knocked you up for the second time, babe.

“I can see that fear in your eyes, thinking I’m gonna go back to that shit once we hit a road bump, but I’m not. Don’t believe me? Ask Pops or Grady. Fuck, ask my own goddamn mother, who I’m guessing doesn’t know shit about her grandkids either. Go ahead and ask any motherfucker that’s been in my life day to day for the past three years. *I. Am. Clean.*”

“I just need time, okay?” Everything he’s saying sounds so perfect, so right. I love the idea of a clean Wyatt. I love the fact that despite how much he was fucking up personally, he handled his shit with the club and made it to VP and—now that he’s clean—president. But that doesn’t mean I feel it in my heart. How the hell am I supposed to just jump back into everything we were when I’m not the same woman?

“You’re either my old lady or you’re the mother of my children. You don’t get to pull away or run from me every time I try to touch you but then turn around and demand more from me when I’m already trying to give you everything I fucking have.”

And there’s nothing else to say. Because as much as I want to be that woman he can fuck and then tell all his dirty secrets to, I’m terrified that she’s the reason he never stayed clean. I can’t do that to him or to my kids, and I really can’t do that to myself. I’ve lost him once already. I can’t fall into us only to lose him again.

CHAPTER FOURTEEN

September 2015
7 months to Mancuso's downfall

It's been two weeks. Two weeks of family breakfasts and family dinners. Someone throws a fit, and someone throws food, and it's an exhausting physical and emotional mess. On the good days, Piper's the guilty party. On the bad days, it's Zander. At least his fits are getting fewer and far between. I try to tell him as much as I can that Wyatt's not going anywhere, but he gets tired of hearing it. Or maybe it's that he's tired of needing to hear it. Either way, it makes him bitchy. So I keep finding new ways to let him know that his dad's here and he's not leaving.

But it's us, and for the first time in forever, we're a family. I'd never say it to my kids—because they're my entire world—but without Wyatt here, there was always something missing. Since the day Zander was born, we've been a family, just him and me. Neither of us knew what we were doing, but we knew we loved each other, and that helped us make it through that first year. I was unprepared, insane, depressed, and probably not a very good mother. But I kept the kid alive, and for a girl who was seventeen at the time, I guess that means something.

I might not know where Wyatt and I stand, but I do know where we stand with our kids. We're their parents. We even headed down to Fort Bragg High School as a family to register Zander. To say the kid's thrilled about Grady's old lady being his student advocate would be an understatement. I think he thinks he's going to get special privileges or something. He won't, but I guess he's got to try. It's such a small thing, but when Wyatt wrote himself down as Zander's dad, my belly got all fluttery. It's just one more thing that tells me he's changed. Maybe one day I'll really believe it.

Wyatt's growing into the dad role really well, and if I'm being honest, it kind of scares me. We've had two weeks of perfect. I know that fucked up is right around the corner, and that makes me uneasy and on guard when he's around. He knows it, too. At first, he was calling me on it, but then he stopped, and I was grateful until I started to worry that it meant he doesn't care if I let him in or not. The two times I tried to talk to him, he blew me off for Piper. I'd be a shitty mom if I got mad about that, so I just kept my mouth shut and walked away.

It's a good thing, I tell myself. It really is. Pip's been buddying up to her dad the way I always imagined she would. It was slow going at first, but now she seeks him out. He's never made it to the house before she has gotten up, but she still wakes up looking for him. The closest he came to seeing her wake up was the morning after she'd been up all night and we'd fallen asleep on the couch. I almost suggested he just stay over after he told me that it kills him that he's never even seen her wake up. And fuck if that didn't just kill me, too. I can't just invite him over to my dad's house, though. Especially not if I don't want him sleeping in *my* bed. I don't think he'd want to anyway, because he's never invited us to his place. I don't even know where he lives.

It doesn't matter.

It really doesn't matter.

All that matters is that I have a free hour to nap while Piper is asleep, and I'm wasting it thinking about Wyatt and worrying about the severe disconnect between us. For the first time since I was eighteen, I'm unemployed and have nothing to do but raise kids. And that means I can take naps—well, when the baby takes a nap I can—but it doesn't fucking matter if I don't actually *sleep* during naptime.

Several deep breaths, a few calming chants, and some major determination to fall asleep later, and I'm dosing off. And it's glorious. I'm right at the place where everything is slowly getting fuzzy and my thought processes are slower than normal, and I don't make sense even in my own brain. Sleep is like a drug when you've got kids. I swear, if a dealer sold it on a corner, I'd be like a goddamn junkie looking for my next fix.

I slowly slip into a quiet, thoughtless abyss.

A loud, obnoxious banging sounds from the other side of the front door. I don't know if I've been asleep for a minute or an hour, but suddenly I'm not asleep anymore. I'm wide awake and fixing to beat somebody's ass. I pull my tired body up from the couch and practically crawl to the front door. My eyes are heavy, my head hurts, my body is worn, and my right index finger twitches to pull the trigger on a gun I'm not even holding. I might not have a gun in hand, but I could go for an old-fashioned ass whooping right about now. So help me God, today is not the day to go to jail. I've got shit to do.

I pull the door open without even thinking about it being someone dangerous. By the time I realize it could've been a threat, it's too late. My vision is fuzzy from my being half-asleep, so I close one eye to better focus only to wish I hadn't. Ryan Stone, Wyatt's new sergeant-at-arms, is standing in the doorway with a pissed-off look on his face. I've known Ryan for most of my life, and he's not only an asshole, but he's a cocky asshole to boot. He's moody, irrational, and, last I checked, a fucking child half the time. I like his dad, Jim, a lot, so I should probably avoid choking his son.

Still, it's a fantasy.

"Moving truck's here," he says shoving past me and into the house. I breathe a sigh of relief and look outside only to find Ruby's red Suburban. The moving truck is nowhere in sight.

"I don't see it."

"Yeah, what I meant to say was the moving truck is at your new house. Your shit will fit in the Suburban, right?"

"New house? Excuse me?"

Just when I'm about to lay into him, a few men I recognize walk through the door. First in is Bear—whose name I only remember because he's one hairy motherfucker—and then Jeremy, who I have on good authority is everybody's favorite prospect. Except for Grady's, of course. The kid reminds me a lot of Wyatt before he got into the drugs and women. He's handsome as hell. No wonder Grady's daughter fell in love with him.

Next in is Diesel. I smile to myself, but it falls when I see the black and purple bruises around his left eye and the bridge of his nose and the large cut on his bottom lip.

"You look a little rough around the edges," I say. He lifts his uninjured eyebrow and grimaces. This ass-beating is obviously fresh. The bruises from when he told Wyatt about what went down with Rig had finally started to fade just a few days ago. And now this. I'm normally of the mindset that brothers fight and sometimes they get some nasty merit badges for their efforts. But this is different. Wyatt's anger is misplaced. He's angry with Rig and himself and even me. Not Diesel. I just hope this fresh set of bruises is from something else.

"Talk to your old man."

Well, there goes that hope. I'm just going to have to talk to Wyatt about laying his anger on Diesel.

"Asshole's got a temper," I say and give him a sad smile. Wyatt losing his shit on him the first time made sense—he'd given him some seriously bad news. And it happened right after Wyatt found out about Zander. But this? This is bullshit.

"Where's Wyatt?" My hands are on my hips, and I'm getting more irritated by the second. Diesel shrugs and wanders into the kitchen where he starts disassembling the highchair with ease. My head falls to the side in wonderment. He's done in half a minute and has moved on to the cupboard where I keep Piper's plastic dishes.

"Up until about a month ago, Chel, Xavier, and I were roommates. Ain't my business how you run your shit, babe, but you should call your sister. She misses you. Needs you now. Your sister and my woman don't get along, and it's driving me fucking crazy—but they both love you." My stomach drops. I haven't seen her since that first day back. I'm such an asshole. So caught up in my own shit, I totally blew her off. It wasn't on purpose, there's just been so much going on and...I don't have an excuse. I just suck at being a good sister. I'm an even worse aunt. I've never met Xavier, but apparently Diesel's stepped up for the kid.

I nod and leave him to the kitchen, deciding that the last thing I want to talk about is Chel. I love her. She's my sister. I just don't understand her, and it makes me feel judgmental, and I hate feeling that way. In the living room, Bear is tossing toys in a trash bag. I remind myself that I could fight this whole moving-to-a-place-I-don't-know thing. It won't do any good, though, and I know that, so I just take a deep breath and go with the flow. If I pitch a fit, Wyatt will show up and threaten to tan my hide in front of the boys. Then Zander will get pissed when he finds out and pick a fight with his dad over it—and he *will* find out even if it's not from me, because he's nosy like that—and that's two relationships that really can't handle the strain. So I bite my tongue and thank God my boy is at school right now.

Heading down the hallway, I note that Dad's bedroom door is open, and thank God he's off doing something I'd rather not think about. Not that he'd interfere with club shit—and this is definitely club shit whether I like it or not—but he's a grouchy motherfucker, and I don't have the patience to deal with his commentary right now. He'd tell me to be grateful that Wyatt's trying and not to fight with him about this moving stuff. It doesn't matter that I came to that decision on my own. I don't want my father telling me to do it. Piper's and my room is at the end of the hall, with Zander's bedroom door just a few feet from it on the right. He hasn't done anything with his room, even though I told him to get comfortable. I realize that, for once, it's a good thing he rarely listens to me as I watch Jeremy take his two duffel bags out of the room with ease and toss them in the living room.

A loud, high-pitched scream comes from my bedroom. I pick up the pace and rush through the open bedroom door at the end of the hall to find the issue. Piper is standing up in her Pack 'n Play with tears falling down her face like a waterfall, holding on to the railing, and screaming at the top of her lungs. My attention shifts to Ryan, who's in the corner of the room frozen in place. One eye is bigger than the other, and he's staring at my kid like she's a two-headed monster—which she sometimes imitates—and holding her favorite stuffed dog in his hand. I weigh my options and decide to make this a teaching moment.

"She doesn't know you, and you have Barky. He's her favorite."

He stares at me stupidly, so I nod to the dog in his hands. He eyes the dog questioningly and walks it over to the portable crib, bends at his knees, and shows it to her.

"It's okay, Pippy," I say in a gentle voice and move to stand next to Ryan, bending at the knee, too. Slowly, the tears stop and all that's left is a crusted mess of boogers and tears on her face. "This is Ryan."

She reaches her little arms out to him and says, "Mine."

"How did Barky get out of your crib?" I ask, putting a hand up to stop Ryan from handing it to her. This throwing the fucking dog out and then pitching a fit about it business has to stop. The kid sniffles and just stares at me with knitted brows and a seriously ticked-off expression on her tiny little mug. I repeat the question and wait for her answer. Zander was a hot mess and was throwing his toys until he was three, but I learned this time. Sometimes I feel bad for my girl that she's second in line and I've learned from raising her brother—she doesn't get away with even half the shit he used to.

"Don't know." Well, she can say those two words almost as clearly as she can say *no*. I'm all about learning and growing as a person, but couldn't she learn something other than sass? That answer doesn't work for me, so I continue to wait.

Finally she tries to tell me some kind of complicated story. At least that's what I'm inferring from the baby babble. It's not really English and makes absolutely no sense, but it sounds an awful lot like an excuse.

"Stop throwing Barky, baby girl," I say and let Ryan hand him over. She sits back down, hugging her dog and babbling to herself.

With the crisis averted, Ryan goes back to packing shit up. I refuse to let him touch my stuff and instead opt for packing it up myself. We didn't bring much with us, just what would fit in my SUV and Elle's stepdad's truck bed. Everything else was put on a big-ass moving truck to arrive later.

I take a deep breath and try to focus on the task at hand. If I think too much about what's coming, I'm going to make myself sick. I just need Wyatt here to tell me where we're going and what's going on. I want him to do that annoying fucking thing he's been doing lately where he kisses my forehead when he sees me. It drives me nuts, but right now I need that contact. Everything keeps changing in my life and my kids' lives, and it's fucking scary. My life was stagnant for years, and now, in a matter of weeks, everything has flipped upside down.

The panic creeps in, sending boulders at my chest, butterflies to my stomach, and a shiver up my spine. I'm trying so hard to hold it together, facing the wall so nobody can see my face and focusing on keeping my breathing regulated, but nothing is working. Finally I resort to the one thing I know will help—Wyatt.

I fire off a quick text with the only thing I need to say: I NEED YOU.

CHAPTER FIFTEEN

It's been thirty-seven minutes and still no response from Wyatt. Jeremy got some kind of call as we were leaving the house to which he told the caller, "She's fine," and then promptly hung up. And now, for the second time this month, I'm being forced to ride as a passenger in my own vehicle. The first time was to prevent an escape, but this time is just stupid.

"Pres told me not to let you out of my sight," Jeremy said when he slid behind the wheel. Much to my dismay, Diesel nabbed shotgun and left me in the backseat with Piper. I could've complained, but it would have gotten me nowhere. I doubt any of the boys would understand what I was complaining about anyway. Ryan and Bear took the Suburban and headed out after us. We've gotten on the highway, and we're heading north into town now. Highway 101 lines the California coastline, oftentimes veering in and out of one small town after another, where it becomes a central street with stoplights and businesses before turning back into a real highway again just beyond the city limits. Before I got too pregnant to ride, Wyatt took me up the coast, and we tooled through at least four small towns before it got late and we headed back. That night he told me something he'd never said before—and something he's never said since—that he was hoping for Baby Z. That's always been one of my favorite memories of California. Actually it's one of my favorite memories ever. It's the only thing that ever pulls me out of the suffocating depression that sometimes kicks in. When Zander was a baby and I could barely get out of bed to care for him, knowing Wyatt wanted him—even if he wasn't there—was the only thing that motivated me to make sure he was well cared for.

"Where are we going?" Zander asks.

I open my mouth to tell him that I wish I knew, but I decide against it. I'm supposed to be the adult here, and adults are supposed to have answers like this for their kids. Zander and I have never been in this situation before. I always keep him tuned in when it involves him. But this isn't my show. This is his dad's shit, and I don't know what's going on. I trust Wyatt to take care of us, though. He would never do anything to intentionally hurt us. I let out a heavy sigh and tell my boy we're going to our new home. I don't want him getting the idea that it's cool to just take over someone's entire life like Forsaken men are known to do, but I'm not going to condemn the club for it either, so it's best I keep my mouth shut.

This situation is entirely new for my little family, so I do my best to put on a happy face. It doesn't work—Zander sees right through it—so I give up halfway to town. By the time we're on Main Street, breezing past a few neighborhoods I could see myself living in, Zander quips that this is basically a kidnapping. Jeremy's jaw tenses, and he eyes my kid like he's fixing to kick his ass or something equally as stupid, but he thinks better of it and just tells Z that it's not kidnapping if you're with your parents. Z doesn't take kindly to Jeremy's attitude, and he spends the rest of the drive giving him a dirty look but wisely keeps his mouth shut. Christ, I have one boy already. I don't need another one on my hands, but it looks like these two are awful keen on giving each other shit, so it doesn't really matter what I want.

By the time I chill a little about the looks Zander and Jeremy are giving each other, I realize that we've already been through town, and before I know it, we're on Sherwood Road. I can't imagine where Wyatt's planned on moving us to, but I just hope it's not too far out of town. It would suck to be out in the middle of nowhere—again.

Much to my surprise, Jeremy slows the SUV and turns down Riverdale Drive. It's been years since I've been out here. I think Zander had just turned six or something when Grady had called, telling me Wyatt was on a bender. He must have been at the end of his rope. He had never called before, and he never has since. The only other time I've been called out to handle my man was when we conceived Piper. That time, though, it was Mishy who called at Ruby's behest. I'd refused that time, but then he went missing, and I gave in. I may hate all the shit he's put me through, but he's the father of my kids. I didn't have to like him or his behavior to help.

Keeping Zander and Piper's dad safe is the absolute least I can do for my kids.

"Thinkin' too much, babe," Diesel says, breaking the silence in the car.

I pull myself from my thoughts and fix my eyes on his. Wide, sympathetic eyes stare back at me the same way they did the day I turned up at the clubhouse to tell Wyatt about Z. I flush in embarrassment. Did my little trip down memory lane worry Diesel that much? The last time he looked at me like this I was in the middle of a panic attack. When I finally tear my eyes from Diesel, I find Zander's body is completely still. He's listening intently even if he appears to be looking out the window.

"Last time I was here, Wyatt had gone off the deep end," I say honestly. I don't lie to my kids, and even if the truth sucks, I'm going to respect Zander enough to give it to him. "I know he's different now. I don't doubt that. Just can't always keep the memories at bay is all."

The tension in the vehicle skyrockets. Zander doesn't move, but his face forms into a glower. I probably shouldn't have said anything. It's an awkward thing, talking about my old man to his brothers, *his men,* but I can't tiptoe around the reality of the situation with my kid. If the guys don't like it, they don't have to listen, much less talk to me. I'm being uncooperative and I know it. I have a responsibility to my kid to protect his heart as much as I can, and part of that means not lying to him about what being an addict means.

Pushing everything else mentally aside, I focus on the road ahead. The ground is a mix of loose gravel and dirt, giving the entire street a quiet, country feel. The homes are even farther apart here than they were before. They're bigger, too. Grady got in on this neighborhood early enough and had the house built the way he wanted it, with some parts—like the garage—not being added on until later, thus making the whole thing more affordable than if he had bought it resale. One thing Dad always preached was investing. He encouraged his brothers to invest their money in something—mostly a house—because no matter how flush money may be at the time, the tides will turn and they'll end up in the hole. My dad's a real asshole, but he's a smart asshole.

"Tell me we're not staying with Grady and Holly." It's more of a demand than a question. I've only met Holly that once at the clubhouse, and she was perfectly nice. They're pretty new, though, even if she is pregnant, and I don't want to feel like an inconvenience. I eyeball Grady's white house warily as we pass it without slowing. Nobody says a word, but I take this as a sign we aren't staying with Grady and Holly. I breathe a sigh of relief and search the street for something small and quaint enough that I think Wyatt would have reasonably rented.

My mood sours as we approach the end of the street. In the distance sits a white farmhouse. The same white farmhouse that's soured my mood to every farmhouse—whether that's reasonable or not—because I once found Wyatt there, slumped over on the house's porch. At the very least, it was empty, so nobody had called the cops.

It's not the house's fault my man chose that exact spot to pass out after overindulging on God only knows what. But it doesn't matter. The image of Wyatt looking half-dead is burned into my memory. It doesn't matter that I used to love farmhouses—and I wanted a white one. It doesn't matter that it's perfectly set on the land, having disturbed as few trees as possible. There's more trees around this home than the rest. The builder must have had a hell of a time keeping all those trees in place. Even Grady, who values his privacy more than almost anyone I know, chopped down a considerable number of trees around his property to make room to build. But not this stupid farmhouse. None of it matters because I still see Wyatt, with shallow breaths, a heart that isn't beating properly, and glazed eyes, staring back at me from that fucking porch.

And it makes me want to burn the goddamn thing to the ground.

Right when I'm in the middle of a full-on hatefest, Jeremy slows the SUV as we approach the house and stops. He then backs the SUV into the farmhouse's driveway, puts it in park, and cuts the engine. Bad memories aside, there's no way I can afford to live in a house like this. If I'm being honest, there's no way I can afford to live in any of these homes. Even the more modest ones. What the hell was Wyatt thinking?

"This isn't right," I say to no one in particular. Because it can't be. The rent on a place like this alone must be at least triple my old little ranch in Detroit.

Jeremy and Diesel ignore me as they exit the vehicle and walk around to the back, where they start pulling out

Piper's mobile crib and setting it on the ground. Zander climbs out, and I unbuckle a sleeping Piper from her car seat. I catch sight of Jeremy tossing a set of keys at Zander and telling him to go explore just as I'm getting us out of the car. Deciding I won't get anywhere with the guys, I follow my boy to the house in silence. He's dragging his feet, but the moment he catches sight of the gleaming chrome-and-black Harley that's set off to the side, he picks up his pace and rushes up the steps with an enthusiasm I haven't seen in days. I bite my tongue when I feel the urge to tell him not to get comfortable.

I've never worked outside of the club before, but I can probably find something in town if I have to. Rig had promised my dad he'd keep me employed in something respectable. I've spent the last thirteen years keeping the books for the strip club the Detroit charter owns. It didn't pay big, but it paid enough to afford the essentials and a few extras. Most old ladies don't work. The club can be a little archaic about that stuff. The brothers like to show they can take care of their own, so it's not something that's done often, but when it is, it shouldn't ever be out of necessity. Christ, even growing up in this shit I can see how outdated it is. Still, Wyatt and I aren't technically together, so I can't rely on him to foot the bill for us.

By the time we're inside, my nerves are totally shot. I make quick work of identifying the dining room to the left and the living room to the right. There's a staircase sidled up to the left wall that separates this space from the dining. Opposite the staircase, the wall dividing the living room and foyer is covered in black frames of various sizes and styles. We get closer only to find that they're our photographs. All arranged nearly the same way they were on our living room wall back in Detroit. My mind races as I find my living room furniture already set up in a way that makes it look like it belongs. The dining room has a plethora of moving boxes, some stacked so high that they nearly tower over me. On the back end of the foyer is a large country kitchen with my kitchen table sitting center stage. To its left is what looks like a mud room and to the right is an open space that might be the family room. There's nothing in there, so I can't really tell what its function should be.

"Where's Dad?" Zander's voice is a mix of accusation and disappointment and booming with teenage theatrics. Piper jolts awake quickly in my arms and stares at her brother in indignation. Her lower lip trembles before she pulls it back and kicks at me to let her down. I lower her to the floor and do the irresponsible mom thing and let her wander off on her own for a minute. She's still sleepy, so she's kind of slow, so I don't feel too awful about it.

Through the wall of kitchen windows that overlooks the backyard, something catches my eye. And when I see what it is, a smile brightens my face. I grab at Zander excitedly and pull him to the windows so he can see what I'm seeing.

Wyatt's barbecuing.

"Your dad barbecues like a fucking boss," I say. We watch as he stands over the grill, a grilling spatula in one hand, a bottle in the other. There's a wooden table and chairs behind him, already made up, waiting for a family of four to join. A brand new highchair sits in place of the fourth chair, and my heart sings at the sight. He's been waiting for us. My stomach rumbles, suddenly in dire need of food. Zander perks up instantly and rushes out the back. I almost follow when I remember I sent Baby Godzilla off on her own, and I go find her before joining my boys in the backyard.

CHAPTER SIXTEEN

Somewhere in the back of my mind, I know I've dozed off during the movie. I don't even care that I'm half-asleep, snoring softly, and with my mouth hanging open. In the background, I can hear the final scene of *Point Break*—the 1990 version, not the remake—on the TV. This is Wyatt's favorite movie. It's actually mine, too. As ridiculous as it sounds, we bonded over our shared love of the brotherhood between Bodhi and Utah. Wyatt used to tease me that I only fell for him because of his excellent taste in cinema. He was half-right, I think. Still, I never kept a copy of it in the house after we broke up. I couldn't stand the idea of seeing it on a shelf, much less watching it without him. So this was Zander's first watch, and it seems like he's a fan.

"What happened to him?" Zander asks. He shifts in his seat, almost elbowing me in the arm before pulling away. The sofa dips, and I slump to the side just before a large warm body—Wyatt's large warm body—pulls me against him. I do my level best not to tense up at the contact and to just go with it. We've had a good day—a really good day. Despite the fact that Wyatt did indeed move us into this blasted farmhouse, he's made a point of making this a home for us. The kitchen already had an assortment of necessities that were brought over from my rental in Detroit, as well as a few new things he'd supplied. There's still a lot of boxes to go through, but he's already done so much.

I'm supposed to be asleep. I really did doze off sometime between Utah and Tyler hooking up and the botched bank robbery, and I didn't come to until Utah was in Australia. Wyatt's deep voice rumbles against my head as the credits roll. "He let him go."

"Did he die?" Zander's voice comes from across the room. My heart warms at my boy's enthusiasm. I was worried the film would be too dated for him, but he's a good egg.

"Probably, but it doesn't really matter," Wyatt says. "What's important is that he got the chance to do something he loves. All men should be so lucky."

There's a long silence between the two that makes me uncomfortable. We had such a great dinner out in the backyard. Even my messy little girl ate the baby burger I made her without protest. Zander kept asking Wyatt how long we got to stay in this house for, and Wyatt kept saying forever. It bugged me, Wyatt telling him that. He can't just promise shit to kids that he can't follow through with. Z will hang onto that like a lifeline, and the minute his dad's promise becomes a lie, it's going to blow up. After dinner, Zander suggested a movie, and with little convincing, Wyatt got us to watch *Point Break*. We wedged ourselves onto the sofa—Wyatt and I on the ends with Zander in the middle—and it was so normal and perfect and right.

Piper even fell asleep on her dad's lap. He held her there until—well, for all I know he could still be holding her. At some point all the perfect family shit just became too much and I closed my eyes. I don't hear her breathing, though, so she might be in her portable crib. I want to worry about where she is. I feel like I should. I can't bring myself to though. She has Zander and Wyatt, so she's safe and taken care of, even if I did fall down on the job. There's this thing that happens with depression. Even when things don't change, they feel like they suck or it's all just numb. Then the really good stuff starts up, and I just can't handle it. It's like every ounce of hope is threatening to spill out and flood the world. And once the hope is out there, I'm raw. There's nothing that can protect me from being destroyed by my dream falling apart again.

"Dad?"

"Yeah?" Wyatt's voice is low and rough. Emotional. About a week ago Zander asked Wyatt what he should call him. It was awkward and sweet and so many things that it broke my heart. My boy never should have had to ask. He should have always had his dad, and his dad should have always had his son. And no amount of feeling like shit is going to give that back to either of them.

"Are you, um…do you…I mean," Zander stumbles over his words.

"You can ask me anything. No joke. You ask, I'll answer."

"Do you like my mom?"

Well, that whole not being tense thing is totally not happening now. My entire body stiffens at the question.

"Fuck," Wyatt says heartily. There's a laugh in there somewhere judging by the shaking of his chest. "Boy, I love that woman something fierce."

"Are you going to live with us? Are you getting back together?"

"We weren't ever not together," Wyatt says earnestly. "You know that tattoo your mom's got on her back? And the one on her shoulder? Those tell the entire world that she's mine. No man will ever have her without seeing *my* name on her skin. Nobody will ever see her body without knowing she belongs to Forsaken. I screwed up a lot, and we couldn't be together back then, but you, me, Pips, and your mom? We're family, and nothing beats that. I live where you live. I sleep where your mom sleeps. She doesn't have to like it, and she doesn't have to let me touch her, but I'm here."

"Too far, man," Zander says in disgust, his voice trailing off. I hold back the snicker in my throat. "A simple yes would have worked. I'm going to go shower now if I can find a towel."

"How do you think you and your sister got here? We certainly didn't make you while in separate rooms." Wyatt's taunting dissolves into full-on laughter. He turns his body into mine, wraps his arms around my waist and legs, and pulls me onto his lap. I try not to stir, but my stillness gives me away.

"You're a shit liar."

I peek one eye open slowly, met by Wyatt's disapproving gaze. My eyes open and close rapidly in an attempt to portray an innocence we both know doesn't exist.

One of his hands finds its way to my chin. He holds it steady so I can't pull away. I shift, only realizing too late it's the wrong thing to do.

"Keep doing that and I'm going to be hard enough to fuck you on this tiny-ass couch." Wyatt's words tumble out all dark and rough but still soft somehow.

"This couch isn't tiny. You're just enormous," I say in defense of my old-ass piece of furniture.

"And you still can't fake sleep. After all these years you still think you can snow me," he says. Very slowly, he leans in and our noses are side by side, our foreheads pressed into one another.

"You told our son we're sleeping in the same bed," I say accusingly.

"We are." His voice is low, his breath heating my skin. I breathe him in only to wish I hadn't. He smells like burgers and root beer—because that's what he had with dinner, a freaking root beer—but underneath all that is his spicy scent that can't be from a soap or shampoo. It's just Wyatt. I've missed it so much that at times it felt like I was suffocating without it. Like if I couldn't remember how he smells, I'd just waste away to nothing right then and there. It never happened—God was never that generous—but it felt real enough that it could be a serious possibility at the time.

Wyatt slides his hand down from my jaw to my chest, laying his palm flat against my heart. His eyes fall closed, and I swear, I think I'm watching him listen to my heartbeat. It's crazy fast now, with the way he's touching me. His calloused fingers press so gently but determinedly against my bare skin. The scoop neck I'm wearing used to have a higher neckline before my kid make it her personal mission to work out by yanking on my clothes all the time. Now, though, I'm grateful for Piper's annoying yanking on clothes, because I can't imagine having his hand over a thin layer of cotton.

"I love you, you stupid woman," Wyatt says softly. His eyes are still closed, prompting mine to shutter closed as well. I breathe him in and keep quiet. I shouldn't give in to this, but I'm a selfish creature. I want my man back if even for a night. Wyatt presses his lips softly against mine. I move into him, but still he doesn't remove his hand from my heart. Our kiss is soft and full of promise and hope, and it absolutely slays me.

Hope is the death of all things.

"If you were done with me, with us, I'd know. Your heart wouldn't be beating this hard. But it is. I'm a part of you, even if you don't want me to be. So yeah, we sleep in the same bed."

I'm scared and furious and trembling. I want to tell him these things. I want to tell him so much, but I don't because he's right. I'm not done with him. I couldn't ever be done with him. I move a shaky hand to his heart, sliding it under his cut and placing it above his worn dark-red shirt. His heart beats at a normal speed that almost infuriates me. How can I be such a nervous wreck and it's like he isn't feeling anything? I open my eyes to find he's watching me with a purposeful gaze.

Love.

It's love that shines back at me. He loves me, and he knows this is right. That's why he's so assured. I don't tell myself that this is forever or that we're fixed. I just tell myself that I'm a woman who needs to feel her man tonight. I tell myself that it's okay not to fight every second. It's okay to give in to what you want even if it might be destructive.

Our lips meet, and this time determination peppers my movements. My tongue swipes against his lower lip, teeth nibbling at the corner of his mouth. I shower my man with all the love I can't bring myself to verbalize. He takes my mouth, just as determined to make a point. I'm not sure what either of us is bartering for, but it feels like the stakes are higher than they should be. I just want tonight. At least that's what I'm telling myself.

Our kiss heats up into something not suitable for a public place—at least not suitable with a teenager walking around. I'm sliding myself over his lap, back and forth, creating the most delicious friction. My body warms from the effort, and I find quickly that Wyatt is enjoying it as much as I am. But it's not enough.

"Upstairs," he grunts through our kiss.

I nod and wait for him to lift me like he used to. From a sitting position straight to standing with little effort. But he doesn't, instead he maneuvers my legs to the side and forces us to each bear our own weight as we move to stand. "Gettin' old, babe."

I don't think of Wyatt as old, not ever, and definitely not while looking at him. But I don't say anything because I'm no spring chicken anymore either. We stand, and he offers me his hand. I take it, and he gently tugs me toward the stairs.

"You haven't seen our room yet," he says with a husky tone. It's laced with a mixture of desire and desperation that sends a thrill through me. Over his shoulder he shoots me a devilish wink. "You should see the place where I'm going to be sinking into your pussy every night."

Instinctively, I grip his hand tighter and don't let up until I can breathe again. A shudder runs through my entire body, leaving me unable to walk. When I don't move, he eyes me over his shoulder again and says, "I want your pussy, babe. Not gonna wait for it."

I flush and let out a shuddering breath.

Holy fuck, have I missed him.

CHAPTER SEVENTEEN

We make our way upstairs slowly and quietly, pausing every few moments to take a deep breath or squeeze each other's hand. He's concentrating hard on something. I can practically see his brain spinning from here, but I don't comment. Whatever he's working through is personal, and I don't want to ruin the moment by making inappropriate comments or saying something that will upset him. It's strange, though, the way he's acting. It's like he's a nervous teen boy who's never done this before. And to be fair, I didn't even get that boy. By the time I met him, he'd already moved past that stage, so this is entirely new to me.

He pauses at the top of the stairs before leading me down the hall to our bedroom. My life feels like some kind of incongruent mash-up of pieces that don't really belong together. It's like there's a very definite line between my life with Wyatt and my life without. I've been without him for so long that I think I forgot what it's like to have him with me. I never want to be in that place again—where I don't automatically know when he's around. Where my body isn't so used to his presence that it searches for him when he's not with me. When the crushing loneliness suffocates me. When the only proof that I was ever loved is the sound of our kids talking. When the only thing I have to hold on to is the desperate hope that one day I'll have him again, if even for just a few minutes.

By the time he opens the door and closes it behind us, I can barely stand to hold his hand. I'm charged, my body racing with need and an electricity I can't ever remember feeling before. It's like being on fire and submerged in ice at the same time.

He gives a small tug on my hand, but when I don't move, he turns around and pulls me against him. We stand there for a long moment, our eyes fixed on each other. His eyes are clear, not glazed over and not red. His pupils aren't dilated, and he's steady-footed. My lower lip trembles as I take in the sight before me. Wyatt Strand has always been gorgeous, whether he was eighteen with a boyish charm and wide-eyed view of the world, or he was a little older and more mature. Now, though, he's something else entirely. For the first time since I got back to town, I think I'm really looking at him. Not even the other day when he told me to look at him did I really see what he was talking about. I've spent the better part of two decades looking at him, seeing the man he is and the man he could be if only he tried.

But right now all I'm seeing is the man he's become. Strong, determined, patient. This Wyatt is everything he ever said he was going to be all those years ago when he took me to bed for the first time.

"What are you seeing?" Crazy-beautiful green-blue eyes stare back at me with an assurance that melts every single fear I've ever had. This is us, and it's right, and nothing can stop me from loving this man. Not even Wyatt himself.

"You." I barely recognize the sound of my own voice. I clear my throat and suck in a shaky breath. Wyatt doesn't ask for explanation, he just slides my shirt up over my head and tosses it aside.

"A white farmhouse with a wraparound porch," he says, his hands traveling over my shoulders and sliding the straps of my bra down with them. His eyes don't meet mine, and his words don't make sense, but I push through the lust-filled fog to try to understand it anyway. Without his eyes, I can't make anything out.

"Eat-in kitchen, two-car garage, nice neighborhood."

"Baby," I say on a plea. My brows pull together despite the heat on my cheeks from the tips of his fingers tracing the top of the cup of my bra. It's old and worn, but he's concentrating on the damn thing like it's made of gold.

He ignores me and goes about dragging his fingers down to the waistband of my yoga pants. They're not sexy in the least. I haven't changed since my nap was interrupted this afternoon. Very slowly, almost tortuously so, he slides his hands inside and back around to cup my ass and pull me flush against his body. The near foot height difference between us gifts me with Wyatt's thick, hard shaft being pressed up against my belly from beneath the confines of his jeans. My fingers find their way to the fly of his jeans, where I have to work extra hard to undo the button before sliding the zipper open.

My plans are destroyed by Wyatt slowly, so fucking slowly, pulling my yoga pants and panties down toward my feet. My body is curvier than the last time we were together, with my clothes not fitting the same way, but he manages to strip me down just fine. His movements are precise, thoughtful. I kick the yoga pants away as he holds me at arm's length. My insecurities spring up out of nowhere, and I hate the way I look all of a sudden. My body didn't bounce back after Piper the way it had with Zander. There are stretch marks along my lower belly and on my inner thighs. My ass is wider, and my breasts aren't nearly as perky as they used to be.

"Been waiting years to get you up here," he says and unclasps my bra. I let it fall to the floor mindlessly and stare up at him in confusion.

"Wy," I say lowly in something between a demand and a question.

When he finally meets my eyes, I busy myself by pulling his jeans down, needing something to distract me from the heaviness in the room. Next I discard his boxers but can't bring myself to break our eye contact long enough to catch sight of his exposed cock. Instead I place one hand on his hip to steady myself and fist him with the other, slowly pumping him. He gulps. A shudder runs through him as he continues to stare at me as if he's trying to will me to understand.

"You wanted a farmhouse, baby. It's yours," he says without a hint of apprehension in his voice. A moan escapes him, his neck muscles flexing, before he can continue. "Promised our boy forever here. I fucking meant it."

"You bought us a farmhouse?" My hand stills as my eyes fill with tears. I take a deep breath and focus on not letting the tears fall. This isn't the man I left nearly three years ago. This is who Wyatt was before the drugs destroyed him.

"Fuck no, baby." His hands find their way to my face. He holds my gaze on him, his voice so low and soft that it gives me butterflies. "I built you a farmhouse. Bought the land and built this place for when you came back to me. Knew it'd happen eventually."

"You," I say, unable to finish my sentence. I'm assaulted by the memory of finding Wyatt on the porch, out of his mind, and mumbling the same thing over and over again. *I thought you'd come back to me.* And at the time it made enough sense, but now it means so much more. He built this place for us—for our family.

"I spent every day I could working on it. Had some help, but told myself I had to earn you back. I was clean for five solid years before fucking up the night before you found me here. Last time I'd used was the day I started work on this place." I open my mouth to say something, anything, but he doesn't let me. He places his thumb over my lips and shakes his head. "Been waiting a long time to tell you this shit, so gimme some time to get it out, will ya?"

I nod my head.

"I was coming for you, whether Z was mine or not. Wanted to make sure shit was secure with the club first, but the second we took out Mancuso, I was coming for my family. You gotta know that once shit got clear, I didn't care if Z was mine. He's yours, and that means he's mine, but fuck if I ain't happy to see myself in that kid. Never knew anyone who looked like me before. You gave me that. Twice. Every ounce and every breath, baby."

Tears stream down my face in waves. Almost fifteen years lost to youthful stupidity, snap judgments, and lies. But here my man is, bearing his soul, talking about being adopted in a way he rarely ever has, and letting me have it in ways my heart can't keep up with.

"I love you." I want to say something beautiful like he has, but I can't get my mouth to work beyond that. He pulls me to him, claiming my mouth with his. Our lips slide over each other's, neither of us trying to dominate. He's gentle but needy. Everything about his kiss wakes me up. When we finally pull apart, it's only because I can't breath and my skin is on fire and I'm ready to explode. The apex of my thighs is damp, and my heart is pounding in my pussy, and he's barely touched me. My hand is still on his cock, but instead of pumping, I'm teasing him with gentle touches and reveling in the velvet softness of his skin.

"Baby, I need you."

His eyes hood at my statement, and his mouth works to get the words out, but he eventually says, "You're my woman and I'm your man, and it's time we start acting like it."

With that, he bends me over the bed behind me, turning my body around and propping me up on hands and knees. I've barely looked around the room, my attention so focused on my man.

Oh, hell yes.

Finally.

Hands knead at my ass cheeks. One long finger trails along the outside of my wet pussy before dipping inside. I throw my head back, and gooseflesh breaks out all over my entire body. Wyatt withdraws his finger and then slides it back in so slowly that I mewl in response. He keeps the movement going, adding another finger and then another. Everything feels amazing and awful because it's not enough. This is my man's favorite position. He can see my brand from here, proof that I belong to him and only him. My body is so electrified by the memories of how wild he gets that a pathetic whine breaks from my chest.

"What was that, baby?" His voice sends a jolt through me, knowing he's playing with me when all I really want is his beautiful, hard cock. My face heats as my temper rises. I've always hated being denied.

"Fuck me, Wyatt," I say, almost shouting. Zander's somewhere up here—I just don't know which room he claimed—so I should try to be quiet, but that's never been an option when I'm with my man.

A hard, fast, and not entirely unexpected hand barrels itself into my ass. I can feel myself starting to lose it, my orgasm building as he starts to lose his patience with my attitude. "Behave, woman."

"Fuck you," I shout, barely able to collect enough breath to muster the words.

His hand slaps at my ass again, this time with more force. I yelp, instinctively jumping away from him, but he grabs my hip and pulls me back. In an instant, his finger is gone and he's impaling me in one smooth move, taking my breath away. My arms shake from the force of him inside me, my body is alight with a fiery desire that makes it hard to breathe as I take him in. One long arm reaches out, fingers trailing against my clit and up my belly, over my breasts, before finally curving up and wrapping around my shoulder. He hovers over my back, never letting us break our connection. Long hair tickles my back. Hot breath covers my skin. He's caging me in, and it's everything I've been waiting for. A soft kiss between my shoulder blades—on the ink that forms his name—is a silent testament to who we are.

He is Forsaken and I'm his woman, and nothing will ever be able to end this shit. Because every ounce and every breath of me is in love with this bossy bastard. Every fiber of my being belongs to him. He's my adolescence and my adulthood, and there is no Amber without Wyatt. The weight of the moment gets to me as tears flood my eyes and fall to the bed in front of me. Years of sorrow and loneliness wash away as he slides out of me and back in so hard and quick that more tears fall. And I know this is something new for us. This isn't who we were when we first fell in love, and it's not who we were the last time we were together. This is better.

Unbreakable.

Because if he tries to destroy us again, I'll kill him myself. I've spent way too many years alone to let him leave me again.

Wyatt stretches me, filling me with his hardness. Pressure builds in my core and spreads a glorious heat through my arms and legs. His hand at my shoulder pulls me against him roughly. Again and again. He's rough and demanding. There is no softness in this. He grunts and moans and curses under his breath as the sound of skin hitting skin echo from behind me. His other hand is on my clit, rubbing in circles. Slow at first and then fast and unyielding. It's all I can do to keep my body up, but then he withdraws completely. Cool air hits my wet, swollen pussy, leaving me throbbing and shaky and breathless. He roars back in so hard I think he might break me. My arms give out, but the arm at my shoulder bears my weight, keeping me in place. His fingers pinch at my clit, and I lose it completely. My pussy clamps down on him with such ferocity that I'm amazed he's still able to move.

"Milk my dick, baby," he says breathlessly as he fucks me with his iron cock, never letting up and not pausing to make sure he's not killing me in the process. My arms and legs tense up before shaking wildly as my orgasm rips through me. At the height of it, I can't even breathe. My face reddens from lack of oxygen, and when I finally get my lungs working again, I'm pretty sure my face is flushed and purple. Sweat beads at my scalp and trails down my forehead, catching around my eyes and mixing with my tears. I'm not crying, not really anymore.

My body just shakes and shivers, and I'm not in control of anything. One more thrust and he changes angles, removing his hand from my shoulder and shoving my face into the bed roughly. I can't breathe, but it doesn't matter. I don't think my lungs work anyway.

He hits me exactly where I need him and twists my clit with a shocking roughness that blankets me in nothingness. I lose time, and the only thing I feel is his warm seed filling me as a hot liquid blasts my thighs and the bed and my man. Wyatt grips me harder, taking everything I've got as I greedily demand everything he can give me.

When we come down, he pulls out and flips me over. My heart sinks as he leaves the bed. He doesn't go far—just to the en suite bathroom where he runs water over a washcloth and brings it back, cleaning me up like I'm something precious. When he's done, he climbs back onto the bed and pulls me up against him. I wrap my arms over his on my belly, holding tightly to him, like if I don't he might float away. We lie like that, not saying a word and holding on to one another, until exhaustion overtakes Wyatt and he's on the verge of sleep.

Just when I think he's completely out, one hand grips my belly in a way that makes me nervous. My body's changed after having kids—especially the second one—with my belly being softer and more rounded. He places a soft kiss just below my ear on my neck.

"When you're ready, I want another one." My face heats and I have to beat back the excitement that flows through me. Before I got pregnant with Zander, he talked about wanting kids. It was always a someday, but then Baby Z came along and Wyatt was so fucking happy it scared me to death. I should be scared now, doubtful even. But in the depths of my soul, I can't lie.

I want another one, too.

CHAPTER EIGHTEEN

October 2015
6 months to Mancuso's downfall

Pass the chocolate." I wave my hand at the arrangement of small paper plates with wedding cake samples on them. There were nine samples when we started, but now we're down to five. Mindy Mercer—the bride-to-be—has already picked the one she wants, so I'm not sure why we're sampling cakes like our opinion matters. The whole thing was very last minute, but I don't turn down free cake. These bitches don't let cake go to waste, either. They're obviously my people.

Alex, Ruby's daughter, slides the plate over to me with a soft smile. I smile right back and then divert my attention to the little slice of heaven. Still, I notice the way she's watching Piper intently. I barely get my fork into the slice before Piper's chubby little hand lands right in the middle and grabs a gooey handful of cake.

With a nod of appreciation, I watch my girl's eyes light up when the cake hits her tongue. "Get it, baby."

She's already a mess from the last piece we sampled, but I'm riding way too high on my dream come true to care. Eight weeks of early morning love making before we have breakfast with the kids. In our house. In the house Wyatt built for us. Every day has felt like a dream with few exceptions. Piper and I wave our boys off as Wyatt drives Zander to school. The first few days after we moved into the house, Wyatt would come home and we would try to get some alone time. It never worked. Piper would scream and cry her temperamental little head off until he gave up. The last time we tried for a post-breakfast fuck session, he was the one to stop it. Instead of crying for me like she normally does, she screamed out for her daddy. And fuck if I've never seen my man abandon pussy so quick before. After that he said we couldn't let her cry it out anymore. And that morning he looked me dead in the eyes and said, "I mean it. Love the kids we got, but I want another one. Not sure I'll ever be done making babies with you."

I'm not ready and won't be for a damn long time, so I said nothing. But fuck if those words didn't make my entire week. I heard them when I'd fall asleep at night and thought of it every single time he'd make funny faces at our daughter. It wasn't until a week ago that I realized how much I want another baby, but how awful the timing is, and how reckless we would be to get pregnant again at this point. So I shut it down and stopped letting myself fantasize about it.

"You like kids?" I ask.

Alex shakes her head in dismissal and avoids her mother's curious gaze, but she answers quickly, saying, "I'm too young."

I look around the table at the women my man's brothers have chosen. I was almost four years younger than Alex when I had Zander, but I keep that to myself. Ruby was even younger when she had Ian. Again though, it's none of my business. I'm certainly not going to push her into procreating with her ass-hat boyfriend.

"She's just being awkward because Trigger keeps asking her to marry him," Nic says bluntly. Nic Whelan is barely older than Alex. She's not really one to talk since she's been refusing to marry Duke until her dad, Butch, a Forsaken brother, is released from San Quentin. Eyeing Nic and then Holly, Grady's woman, I spot a rather peculiar pattern when I look around the table.

"Interestingly enough, Ian's the only one here aside from good ol' Jim who's gotten his woman to agree to marry him," I say with a raised eyebrow in Nic's direction.

"Hey," Holly says, finally piping up. "Grady and I are getting married. Now's just not the right time." We're doing this little wedding prep shindig in her and Grady's house, but she's been eerily silent the entire time. Mindy's her cousin, I'd have expected her to be much more excited about this crap than she is.

"What does that mean?" Mindy shoots Holly a dark look. It seems there's some family tension here. I'm dying to know what's going on. I could almost scream at Wyatt for leaving this out. I wouldn't know any of the Forsaken family gossip if it weren't for my man and his chatty post-coital ass. Even Elle, my best-fucking-friend minds her goddamn business, much to my chagrin. Speaking of Elle, I wish that bitch would show up to these things instead of busting her ass on whatever it is she's been working on.

"Don't get an attitude with me," Holly says. In the distance, Robin, Duke and Nic's eight month old baby, starts crying. Nic quietly thanks god and heads off to fetch her daughter.

"Not everything is about you." Holly's follow-up remark has Mindy dropping her plastic fork.

"You think this is a bad time for us to get married? Well, what about you getting knocked up? On purpose?"

Leaning across the table, I glare at Ruby and hiss, "Do something."

"Fuck that," she says with a smirk. "You can handle this, Queen Bee."

I shoot Ruby a look that says this is anything but cool and try to figure out how to calm the Mercer women down. Mindy is one dark bitch who might actually have sicker than her man, but Holly is conniving and ballsy as all hell. On their own, neither woman is likely to back down.

"I get why you're upset, but you can't keep taking it out on me," Holly says with one hand slamming down on the table and the other rubbing her small bump. Mindy's eyes shoot to Holly's belly and soften just slightly. It's only a second though, before they narrow again and turn cold.

"It's not my choice, okay?" Holly shouts frantically. Piper squirms in my lap and covers her ears with her chocolate covered little hands. I snap my fingers to catch Holly's attention and point at Piper. The crazy pregnant lady softens immediately. "I told him this was a bad idea. Grady won't marry me until the club gets back from New York, now just shut up."

"I'm sorry, what?" My voice is tight and the tension in the room rackets all the way up. Even Nic, who's returning with Robin, is avoiding my eyes. Alex is looking at her mother, Nic is focusing way too intently on the wall behind my head, and Mindy is picking at her piece of cake. Holly's covered her mouth with her hand and has lowered her head. Only Ruby has a straight face, way too even for her to not know what's going on.

"Somebody better start talking," I order. Wyatt doesn't talk about the club or whatever has got him so stressed. I keep hearing murmuring about New York, but it always dies down quick the second I walk into the room. The last time I asked ended with Wyatt telling me not to show up at the clubhouse without permission first. He gave me some bullshit about Segreti and safety, but I could tell he was full of crap. We fought about it, but the argument ended quickly when I noticed the bulge in his jeans that hadn't been there a minute beforehand. It's shameless how easily we fall back into the same patterns. Not this time though. I'm done letting him control the conversation.

"All I know is Jim's been evasive about the club since he stepped down," Ruby says.

"Ian doesn't talk to me about it, but something is going on. He keeps preparing for a trip, securing the house and showing me where to hide when he's gone if anybody shows up." Mindy finally meets my eyes, worry overtaking her pale face.

"Damn it," Holly says more to herself than the rest of us. She scrubs at her face before lowering her hands to the table and staring at her hands, brows pulled together in deep thought. "The club took a vote. Once Mancuso is released, they're taking the fight back to New York."

"How do you know this shit?" Holly's silence speaks volumes. So do the looks from the rest of the old ladies. Ruby knew, judging from the look on her face, but the rest of them didn't. Nic's annoyed, Mindy looks like she finally understands what's going on, but it's Alex whose expression kills me. Her big brown eyes are filled with sadness, and her lower lip is jutted out.

"I didn't know," she says and pauses before taking a deep breath. "Ryan told me they'd be leaving once my dad was released, but that was it. I begged him to talk to me, but he wouldn't. I just assumed every one of us got the same speech. I've tried to talk to him, but he won't listen to me."

"No, I didn't get any fucking speech," I say coldly. The wheels turn in my head as I piece the day together. Piper and I were chilling at home when Holly called, inviting me over for a cake testing. It was the first I'd heard of it, but since we live down the street now, I figured it wasn't a big deal to pop over for free cake. Then Holly's weird silence at the get-together she's hosting, and the blow-up between she and Mindy…

"Who did you tell this was a bad idea to?" The hairs on my arms stand straight up as I ask the question. Somehow, I already know the answer. The other day, Zander came home from school and said Wyatt had asked Holly for some kind of favor. At the time, I brushed it off. My boy has had a difficult time adjusting to his new school, and with Holly being a guidance counselor, I figured it had something to do with his grades or sometimes rather rough social skills.

But I was wrong. I can see that now.

"Nevermind," I say when Holly's eyes won't meet mine. She sighs heavily, pushes back from the table, and leaves the room. The anger I expect to flood my vision never comes. Instead, an ice cold determination settles in my gut and spreads throughout my body. I stand and walk Piper over to Ruby. Handing her over wordlessly, I leave the house, trusting that my kid's in good hands with Ruby.

It doesn't take long for me to get back to the house, hop in my SUV, and head to the clubhouse. That wasn't a bonding session with the girls, it was a distraction to keep me out of club business. That's the last fucking time I let Wyatt pull the wool over my eyes.

When I get to the clubhouse, Jeremy doesn't want to let me past the gate. It isn't until I remind him that he can't touch me, and slither past his muscular frame, that I make it through the gates.

"You're kind of an asshole," he says, with his hands in the air and keeping as much space between us as he can. A smile finds its way to my face.

"You haven't seen anything yet, baby boy." Jeremy smirks, all knowing and taunting, like the fucking kid has something on me. I shake my head and turn toward the clubhouse. Stopping dead in my tracks and surveying the parking lot, realization dawns on me. *This* is why Jeremy's being so smug. The lot is full of sleek, black luxury cars and SUVs. *Mafia black.* These fuckers are so predictable. I turn back to Jeremy and decide that being nice might have its perks.

"Friend or foe?" The kid stares at me blankly before blinking. Shaking my head and abandoning any pretense of being in a decent enough mood to socialize and study the clubhouse. I know the way Forsaken men think well enough to know that the front door is locked. The boys won't risk any interruptions when they have visitors—especially not potentially unfriendly visitors.

"You have keys," I say to Jeremy. He stares at me blankly before a cocky grin appears on his face. He's smart and determined. I can see the look on his face. He wants his top rocker more than he wants his next breath. I respect the kid even if he has suddenly come down with the inability to speak. "Cough "em up, prospect."

With narrowed eyes and a casually defiant expression that tells me he's been fighting authority figures his entire life, he closes the distance between us. He's just barely taller than Zander, but that won't last for long. With the rate my boy's growing, Zander will be dwarfing Jeremy within the year. Still, Jeremy Whelan has a muscular weight to him that Zander is lacking, so when he gets almost close enough to touching me, I jump back. I'm used to Zander getting in my face and me having to put him ass where it belongs, but this is different. There's a danger that radiates off Jeremy that I don't expect at his young age.

"Got orders to keep you in the parking lot should you show up. Also got orders to tackle your ass and haul you back out should you find a way into the clubhouse. That shit comes from your old man, so if you don't like it, talk to him." He flashes his brilliant dark blue eyes and his large white smile. "Thanks for keeping me company, babe. It was getting boring out here."

I suck in a haughty breath and turn away from him. He's going to make a damn good brother. I have no doubt they'll patch his ass in when the time comes. Wyatt says he talks to Butch, Jeremy's dad, regularly and the man couldn't be prouder of his boy. From where I stand, he's got a lot to be proud of.

We wait like that, in silence, for a damn long time. I don't even know how much time passes. Only that the sun begins to set and the temperature drops enough to chill me to the bone. I want to ask Jeremy what's going on and who's inside. It seems that if the boys welcomed their visitors into the clubhouse, then they have to trust them on some level, so it can't be Segreti. At least, I'd be damn surprised if it was, but I know better than to bet against these men. Forsaken men pride themselves on being crazy ass fucks who push limits at every turn. There's no telling what kind of deal they're cooking up in there. One thing I know for certain though, it's about New York.

The front door of the clubhouse swings open, the hinges squeaking under protest, and out walks Wyatt with a man—a mafia man—I've never seen before. The man at Wyatt's side is wearing a slick black suit with a white shirt underneath. All perfectly normal and tailored with a dash of personality in the blood red tie at his neck. His ice blue eyes catch mine and a feral smile creeps to his lips. I narrow my eyes in response to the way his eyes rake up and down my body. This man doesn't look Italian, but there is something uniquely European about the way he carries himself. With sandy brown hair, and defined cheekbones, and a long straight nose above a square jaw and thick neck, he's attractive alright. Not my type, but attractive. I don't like my men better groomed than me and save for the beard covering the lower half of his face, he's as clean cut as a whistle. He's all business, while still somehow all about pleasure. It unnerves me to my core to have him staring at me the way he is.

"Mr. Strand, introduce me to your club's woman," he says with a thick Russian accent. One step forward has Wyatt standing between us. My man's large hand is splayed out on the man's chest. He looks down at Wyatt's hand and waits until he removes his hand. The man reaches up very slowly and smooths out his clothes as if Wyatt had sullied them somehow. He didn't, but it's a show of dominance. Intricate tattoos peek out from beneath the arms of his suit. Wyatt doesn't take the bait, he just clears his throat, getting the man's attention.

"Come here, baby," Wyatt says, ushering me over. I move to stand beside him and he tucks me into his side and holds me tight against him. "This is *my* woman."

"Dominik Petrov." The man's eyes fall back on me appraisingly. His words slide off his tongue in a way that can't be anything but natural for him. His eyes don't leave mine when he says, "You're a lucky man."

"Amber Strand," I say with a nod and a steady chin. Wyatt's fingers dig into my side. He likes the way I sound with his last name.

He's not the only one.

Pushing my luck, I smile at Dominik and extend a hand to shake his. He takes my hand in his large one. For such a put-together man, his hands are rough and dry, obviously not cared for in the way the rest of him is.

"Tell me what business you have with my man and my club."

Dominik's eyes flash excitedly, but he remains silent. I know men like him. They don't take kindly to women poking into their affairs. My daddy and granddaddy could tell him stories about trying to keep me out of club business. My granddad, Clutch, got his name for always coming in clutch in difficult situations. At least that's the current party line. My mom used to tell me it was for something entirely different that I didn't want to know about. Clutch used to tell me he was going to beat the shit out of me for speaking my mind. He never did though. My lax childhood can certainly be to blame for this situation. Women don't talk like this—at least they don't do it and get away with it—not in Forsaken and definitely not in the Russian mafia.

Dominik's eyes leave mine in favor of Wyatt, and it's only now as he's dismissed me that I realize how attractive he really is. Enemy or not, if I didn't have Wyatt, I'd consider Dominik Petrov for a little fun. Wyatt's arm that's wrapped around me tightens uncomfortably in warning. Looking up at my man, I give him a soft smile that he snarls at. It's my fake smile and he knows it.

"Bike. Now," Wyatt barks out, releasing me. For once in my life, I follow the order and go to stand beside Wyatt's Harley. In the distance, I can hear Wyatt and Dominik exchanging chauvinistic bullshit retorts. I choose to let them have their fun. My comment did exactly as it was supposed to—it put my man on notice that hiding things from me is going to stop.

CHAPTER NINETEEN

Wyatt lumbers toward me, his now short hair stock still despite the wind that swirls around us. It was just last night that he brought me a pair of scissors and told me to cut it off. I didn't know what to do with that, but I did my best to cut his hair down to just a few inches. "Fresh start, babe," he had said. I can't say I miss the longer hair. It was always a mess and reminded me too much of the old Wyatt.

Wyatt's bulking muscles practically explode from his black shirt as he stomps toward me. His chest rises and falls quickly, like he's willing himself to calm down. I bite at my lower lip, eyes affixed on his, and practically squirm while I wait to wrap my body around him. His eyes hood as he catches sight of my lower lip between my teeth, then he swings a leg over his bike and starts her up. I climb on and wrap my arms around his waist. The deep, loud growl of the bike vibrates beneath me, electrifying my entire body. I lean in, running a hand over the crotch of his jeans as we pull out of the parking lot and head through town.

The first time I did this, I was maybe sixteen years old. Wyatt must have been eighteen or so and he nearly crashed his bike. Now though, as adults with a teenage son, he keeps the bike steady as we leave town and turn off the main road. The area is desolate, on the outskirts of town along Highway 101. By the time Wyatt stops the bike, the bulge in his pants is larger and firmer. I smile to myself, eyeing our surroundings and deciding that if I'm going to be punished for stepping out of line, I damn sure better earn it. Climbing off the bike, I backup toward the tree line to give myself at least a little covering. Turning off the engine, and moving to stand beside the bike, Wyatt fixes his eyes on me.

"When were you going to tell me about New York?"

"Fuckin' Holly," he mutters and takes a step closer, but I put my hand up to stop him. Shocking me, he freezes in place. I'm not used to having my man listen to me. The sudden power energizes me. Holly Mercer and I are going to have some words later. A lot of words and we're going to be having them without either of our men around. I won't hit her—she is pregnant after all—but Grady still won't let me around her if he senses how pissed I am. No reason for our men to fight out an issue that' strictly between us women.

"Who do I belong to?" It's a demand, not a question.

"Me. You belong to me." His voice is rough. Good. The more he wants me, the easier this will be.

"Then fucking act like it." My words are punctuated with my anger. His eyes narrow to slits as he glares down at me. I lift my shirt above my head and place my hands on my hips. His hooded eyes travel down to my breasts. "I am as much Forsaken as you are, if not more. Do *not* hide things from me."

"I'm protecting you," he says on a roar. "You, Zander, and Piper are my entire fucking world. I just barely got the three of you. I won't let this shit touch you."

He takes another step closer. My fingers tingle to touch him, but I keep the feeling at bay long enough to sort this out.

"You and your brothers are fucking idiots if you think keeping your women in the dark is the way to win this war. I haven't been here very long but even I can see where things went wrong, why people have been hurt, and even killed."

"Shut your fucking mouth." He's snapping now, charging toward me, and scooping me up in his arms. My head is shoved against his chest, and just like that, I feel at home. It doesn't matter that we're in the middle of an argument. Wyatt's hard body wrapped around my softer one settles me in a way nothing else ever has. Not even holding our newborn children, seeing them open their eyes, and take one of their first breaths, can ever do. Those memories are laced, after all, with an everlasting sorrow that creeps into the edges of even my happiest memories when Wyatt wasn't there. My beautiful babies both came out so healthy and strong and so very, very precious, but I couldn't fully enjoy the moment as I wanted to. Neither time. My man should have been there. He should have seen their first breath, and first smile. He should have known them from the moment they entered this world. And he wasn't there because life is unfair and cruel and addiction is a vicious beast I wouldn't wish on anybody. Only here, with Wyatt holding me do I ever feel all that pain and anger wash away.

"You have to talk to me," I say quietly. I turn my head and place a kiss to his neck. His chest rumbles in approval.

"You don't know the shit we've been through," he says, lowering us into the grass at our feet. He sits with his legs spread, me between them, close to his chest, but at a good angle to meet his eyes. "Everything has fallen apart in the last two years. We lost Chief, and then Tall—a kid we were going to patch-in. Everything that went down with Nic and her fucking ex? Then the hell that came after we thought we took care of that."

He sucks in a slow, unsteady breath. I don't take my eyes off his face as he chews at his lip. My man's gorgeous blue-green eyes deepen as he works through what he wants to say.

"We had to remove Chief from the grass in front of Jim's place. Buried him and almost lost Grady in the process. He'd basically lost his father. We found Alex in a warehouse, watching her own fucking brother beat the shit out of her. That girl was such a bad fucking idea. We shot up her dad's house and took her away like removing her from New York was going to fix shit, but it didn't. And I hated the sight of her for a damn long time. Every time I looked at her face, all I could see was Chief, dead in the grass. Everything we've done after that has been to protect our family and we've fucking failed at every turn. So no, I don't want you involved in the club."

"All that stuff happened and you stayed clean," I say quietly. It's not more important than Chief—my best friend's father, nor is it more important than the boy who took a bullet to the back of his head while trying to keep Holly and Mindy safe. It's not even more important than Michael Mancuso wailing on his sister who happens to be half his size. I wasn't here to live through every awful day the rest of them have. I can barely imagine how bad it's been, but I know the details. I know the reason Mindy doesn't sleep through the night, and why Holly is so attached to Ian even though she's with Grady. And I know that my man has never dealt with trauma well. The first time he went off the rails was when he met his dad for the first time at nineteen. It wasn't just bad, it was awful. I didn't know he could be that cruel or hate himself that much. One fight when I'm eight months pregnant, one stupid lie he never should have believed, and we broke up. Not five minutes later and he has his dick down some bitch's throat.

One thing I know for certain about Wyatt Strand is that he doesn't deal well when shit hits the fan. And maybe my man staying clean isn't as important as everything else the club has gone through over the past two years, but it is to me. It is to my children. Because while we weren't here, dealing with the hell the Fort Bragg charter has been through, I know my man. And now, without a single doubt, I know he's going to stay clean. Because if he can deal with everything else, he can and will stay away from all the shit that tried to destroy us all those years ago.

"Yeah, I guess I did."

"How'd you do it?" Wyatt levels me with a flat expression. I reach up and cup his face in my hands. His growing beard is rough beneath my touch and tickles at my fingers, but I don't waiver. I prod, asking him again.

"All that shit, all those pills, and lines on mirrors never did dull the pain. All it did was drive you away. I knew, somehow, that Z was mine, but he deserves better. I'm just a piece of shit biker without an education and a rap sheet that would kill several trees to print out. But every fucking day, especially now that you and our kids are here, I remind myself that there's something to live for. I just had to get sick and tired of being sick and tired first. And then it was easy, letting myself be selfish enough to want you and work on my shit so maybe, one day, I could have you."

"You're not a piece of shit," I whisper, pulling myself closer. "Clara's your mom, not because she had to be but because she chose you. I'm your woman because I chose you too. Zander and Piper didn't get to choose you, but I know damn well they would if they'd had the choice."

"You're still in trouble for that shit you pulled back there," he grumbles, his voice softening. I smile up at him and kiss his cheek.

"You can spank me later if it makes you feel better."

"What would make me feel better is you keeping your cute fucking nose out of club business."

I sigh. That's not going to happen. Growing up, I remember my dad confiding in my mom and asking for her help all the time. The Detroit charter rarely made a move without Cindy Wallace having a hand in it. My grandpa, Forsaken's founder, and my grandma were the same way. Mary Wallace, my grandma, is the reason Forsaken only gives out the old lady title after their women have been unanimously voted in by every member of their charter. She did it for a reason—she didn't want brothers sharing state secrets with some bitch they'd drop the next day. Grandma's a smart lady. You protect the patch, you protect the family. Best way to protect both is to be selective about who wears the warrior tattoo and who rocks the patch.

"We need to have another history lesson?" He shrugs me off, but I don't let it get to me. Instead, I move back onto my knees and place my hands on the tops of his thighs. My man needs a little love right now. Licking my lips in anticipation of his sweetness, I reach out and pull down his zipper. He leans back on his hands and appraises me.

"The old ladies exist for a reason. You remember Bloody Mary, don't you?" My voice is light and playful as I pull his hard cock out of its confines. I tease the base with the tips of my fingers while referencing my grandmother and the nickname she earned during Detroit's war with a club in Toronto.

"Babe, please don't talk about your grandma with my dick in your hand," he says on a laugh. There's a smile in his eyes and voice that wasn't there a minute ago. I wrap my hand around his cock and slide it up and down with a smile on my face. I wonder if he can see it—the love

I feel for him. How much I want him and not just now, but forever? Does he know how broken I was before? How much it pained me to be away from him?

Wyatt reaches out and wipes away the wetness in my eyes. He gives me a smile that I know nobody else gets. This is mine. He smiles differently at our kids, especially our daughter. But those smiles are a little brighter. My smile is something more grounded. A little deeper, no less important. Just beautiful and strong and it means so fucking much that I can't even put it into words. After all these years, so many of them apart, and all the damage we've each suffered, I still get this.

"Why are you sad, Mugs?"

I could tell him the truth. All the happy, sappy shit that's going around in my head, but that takes us off course, so I don't.

"Bloody Mary earned her name for single-handedly saving half of Detroit during the Toronto war. I know you remember this shit, but I think you've forgotten why it's important. You do *not* run into battle without your woman by your side. You do *not* treat me like I'm something precious and defenseless."

"Babe," he says, but I narrow my eyes at him and squeeze his dick enough so that he stops and freezes.

"Not wise to piss off a woman when she's got your dick in her hand," I warn and go back to my speech. I continue my ministrations on his dick, using the precum to spread it around the tip, and lick my lips. His dick twitches in my hands and I smile. "I'm only your woman because you earned me. You have the privilege of belonging to me and I have the honor of being yours, but do not underestimate the bitch you belong to or what I'm capable of. Not ever."

Before he can say anything, I lean down and take him into my mouth. It's a dirty trick, sucking his dick so he won't argue, but it's incredibly effective. It doesn't take long for his body to tense and his breathing to be labored. I wish I could see him, but from this angle, it's impossible. All I can see is my name, inches above his dick, right at the top of his light brown curls, as it stares back at me. I know the signs that he's about to come even though I can't see his face. I sneak a hand into his boxers and gently cup his balls as I take him to the back of my throat and moan around his cock. Thick, warm liquid fires into the back of my throat. I greedily suck it down and when he's done, I made a show of licking my lips and swallowing. He grabs me roughly, pulling me onto his lap. His still wet cock dampens the crotch of my jeans. I buck into him and watch as his lazy expression heats up.

"Tell me I'm coming to New York."

He's silent, but I don't rush him. While I wait for my man to come to the inevitable conclusion that he's going to give in, I rub myself against him. His dick softens only halfway and stays like that before slowly hardening again.

"I miss your dick, baby. I want you inside me." He attacks my mouth, kissing me roughly. A slow, quiet fire slowly builds as I continue to rock against him. He clears his throat and moans softly.

"You're a manipulative bitch." Despite the words he uses, his tone is soft. There's no heat behind the statement. Another sign that he's coming close to giving in. "You gonna withhold pussy until I give in?"

"No," I say and take a deep breath. "But I'll make you a deal. You take me to New York and when we get home, I'll give you another baby."

"Fuck," he says quietly. His eyes search mine, like he's making sure I'm not lying to him. Family means everything to this man. Even when he was fucked up, he loved what we had and wanted our son. He was just too sick to be good for himself, let alone us.

"I love you, baby. I just want the father of my children safe and sound and at home with me."

There's a long, frustrated pause before he concedes. I can see it on his face when he says, "Christ, now Ruby's going to want to come. You do realize you just fucked me with the boys, right?"

CHAPTER TWENTY

Wyatt

February 2016

2 months to Mancuso's downfall

"This isn't necessary," Zander whines from beside me as he watches the baker work her magic on the cake. Amber thinks I'm crazy, but I swear the kid's grown in the last three months. I've measured him so many times that any time he sees a measuring tape now, he turns heel and rushes the other way. He's fourteen, so he won't say it, but I know he likes the attention. I remember being fourteen and wanting nothing more than to have a dad. I used to think even a shit dad would be better than no dad. Sure, this shit right here embarrasses him to no end, but deep down the little fuck loves it.

"Is this right?" The baker, a young girl around nineteen or so, turns the cake toward us. She gulps nervously as we stare down at her work. Once again, she's done a good job. The cake she's just finished was a last minute addition to our order. My boy's birthday was back in July, but I wasn't there. Not for his fourteenth or his thirteenth.

Not for any of those fucking milestones. Either I had a straw up my nose, my dick in some strange pussy, or I was already passed out to the point of oblivion. One of the very things I remembered through all that shit I put my body through was his birthday. I think I remembered him being mine too, but I couldn't bear the thought of facing it. Not if she was going to lie to me again and not if I was wrong. Even at my darkest point, the idea that maybe she was wrong or lying and he was mine after all, kept me alive. Only fucking thing, if I'm being honest.

I nod my head and tell her it's cool—because it is. Piper's cake has some kind of pink pig character on it. Amber ordered that shit. If it were up to me, her birthday cake would look a lot like Zander's—white and black with red icing piped atop the chocolate cake and vanilla frosting. The baker is talented as fuck. I asked her if she could draw a Harley on the damn thing and she fucking did. I even got her to draw Forsaken's Nordic warrior in the corner with HAPPY BIRTHDAY, Z written at the top of the Harley. Zander mutters a few words of indifference and hops from foot to foot, but I can see the excitement in his eyes. Cheyenne, Grady's daughter, comes home from culinary school today. She's going to be damn pissed when she sees I had somebody else bake for us—especially when she sees the Forsaken symbol on it—but the girl doesn't have time to be whipping up shit for us. Plus, Grady *still* hasn't told her that Holly's pregnant and they need time to connect and shit. I don't know that he will drop that bomb right now since Holly's been spotting, but he fucking should. Chey's a tough girl—has to be to be in love with Jeremy—she can handle it.

"Great, I'll just pack both cakes up and you're good to go." She shoots Z a sly smile that leaves a blush on her cheeks. I spy my kid's reaction to it. He smirks at her like he's the grown ass man that he isn't and leans in, saying as smooth as fuck, "Thanks, babe."

She blinks at him, blushes again, and rushes off to get the cakes ready to go. I stare at my son with a mixture of pride and shock in my heart.

Memories of being only a few years older than him fly through my brain. I was eighteen the day I met his mom, also the first time I kissed her, and the day I walked up to Thumper-Fucking-Wallace and told him I wanted to prospect for his club and I wanted to make his daughter my girl. Looking back, I'm surprised Thumper didn't murder my ass on the spot. I'm even more surprised that Amber's mom didn't beat my ass for it. I guess they figured any kid that ballsy and stupid was worth taking a chance on. It wasn't long after we met that I started prospecting. She gave me her virginity the day I started earning my top rocker. I was the thing every parent of a teenage daughter fears.

Fuck.

Karma sure is a bitch and if Piper grows up to be anything like her mother, I'm in for some major trouble. I have to fight my every instinct to keep my mouth shut and not tell the kid that we're about to have a talk about wrapping his dick. I'll just lay that shit on him later tonight so when he's all grossed out and pissed off he can do it in his room alone and not let his grouch fuck up his sister's party.

"I can't believe you had everybody sing '"Happy Birthday'" to Z," Amber says. Her body shakes with laughter in my arms. I hold her tighter and place a soft kiss to her cheek.

"Did you see Pip's face?" I ask, laughing at the memory of our daughter realizing that she had to share her birthday. She's only just turned two yesterday, but we spent the entire week telling her that today was going to be her day. I guess she didn't appreciate us throwing some celebrations in there for her brother. She shook her little fist at Z and said, "Not you."

"She's been like that since the day she was born. Bossy and defiant." Amber's voice is wistful, but her message is clear—it's a clear warning for what's to come.

"We need another boy to help keep an eye on her," I say sagely. Last month, after Amber promised we could have another baby if I take he to New York, it's all I've been able to think about. When she was pregnant with Zander, I couldn't keep my hands off her belly. Maybe I'm just a sappy fuck, but seeing her body grow and change with our son was fucking precious. I love Clara—my adopted mom—she was the only family I had until Amber. But it's different. I don't see myself in her features. I don't know where I got my temper from or my size. As far as parents go, my mom is pretty freaking awesome. Even the shit I do with the club doesn't faze her. She still looks at me the same way she did the day she brought me home—with love and respect. But with my kids, I see their eyes and know they belong to me. I see their tempers and know that's on me, too. Except when Piper flys off the wall into a total batshit meltdown—that's her momma. But these two incredible people are mine. I know it in my blood and bones. If they get sick and need blood, I can give it. If they ever find themselves scared or worried, they know their daddy will be there. I'm doing my fucking best to give them every goddamn thing I never had.

"Oh, right. Because she doesn't have enough cousins and uncles," Amber says with a laugh. "We both know she'll always have the club."

"Doesn't mean I don't want another boy," I say. My hands travel down to her belly and rub the empty space with soft circles. Across the park, I catch sight of my mom who's heading toward us. Things have been chilly between her and Amber so far—and for good reason—but I'm hoping the two women can keep their shit silent for at least today. Amber tenses when she spots my mom. I can practically feel her narrowed eyes.

"I liked the cakes—especially Zander's," Mom says as she approaches. She has a smile plastered on her face, but it doesn't quite reach her eyes. I get that she's still not over missing out on fourteen years of grandbabies, but she seems to completely ignore my fault in the situation. I fucking hate being stuck between the two of them. Even Amber understands her frustrations, but there's only so much attitude someone can take before they lose their shit, whether it's deserved or not.

"My man did good," Amber says with a nod. The jab is subtle, but it's there. Mom's eye twitches in response. I give Amber a little squeeze to remind her that I'm here and it's okay. And if I'm being honest, it's also a silent plea to keep her mouth shut. Caving to my request, she softens her voice and says with a genuineness that she was previously lacking, "I'm really glad you're here, Clara."

"I'm glad I was invited." Now Mom's eyes are narrowed on me. "I don't get enough time with my grandkids."

"Lay off, Ma. I need a solid bond with my kids and that takes time. You of all people know that."

Mom's lips turn up into a gentle smile as she appraises me with a nod.

"All issues aside, I wouldn't be opposed to another grandbaby. One I can spoil from birth this time."

"All issues aside, you're a great grandma and our kids are lucky to have you," Amber says, her voice on the edge of an insult. Shit. I thought dealing with Thumper's anger over all this shit was bad, but it's nothing compared to two momma bears fighting it out over their cubs.

"After New York," I say. My promise is clear and the shudder than runs through Amber's body tells me that she recognizes it as just that. I've been promising her another baby after we get back from New York—and by we, I mean the club. The mother of my children isn't stepping foot outside of Fort Bragg. I just haven't told her that I still don't plan on taking her with me. The boys and I—mostly—agreed that it's best that our old ladies stay behind. That way, just in case anything goes wrong, our kids have one parent left. There was a bit of disagreement over the decision—especially from Ian—but he didn't push the subject.

It's different for him. Mindy can't have kids. He's not a father. His woman is still healing from the shit she went through and she's doing it in a seriously fucked way. He can't possibly understand what he'd be asking the rest of us to agree to. Holly is a fighter and so is Alex. But they still carry the emotional scars of what they went through. And Nic has a baby. There's no way in hell that Duke would ever let her leave their daughter. It would be too complicated and far too messy on a personal level to bring a single woman on the trip. Not even Ruby is coming. It's a dick move—letting our women think they're coming with us—but it's better than fighting it out with them until we leave.

My eyes scan the park, searching for my baby girl. My body settles when I find her. She's running around with a cake smeared face and a little baby bullhorn in her hand. She's spent most of the day following Zander around until he got boring and she locked her traitorous little eyes on Jeremy. I don't know what it is about the fucking prick, but the girls love him. The moment Piper ran up and blew the bullhorn at him, Jeremy had bent down and scooped her up in his arms and tickled the hell out of her. The look Chey gave him set off alarm bells in my head, making it impossible to stifle the laugh that erupted when I noticed Grady watching her with alarm as well. The girl has another year left of school before she's home for good, but judging from the way she's checking out Baby Boy, it won't be too long before she makes Grady a grandfather. Fuckin' kids.

"Daddy!" Piper screams from where she's standing by the slide. My first instinct is to check that she's okay and when I determine that she is, I loosen my hold on her momma and kiss her head. With a soft pat to my woman's ass, I head over for our daughter. She tries to convince me to take her down the slide, but when I try to fit at the top of the play structure, it creaks and moans in an unhealthy fashion and I give up the feat. Instead, I offer to hold her hand as she slides down herself. We repeat this act again and again until she gets tired of me and toddles off to find somebody new and more interesting, likely somebody who can fit on the slide without breaking the damn thing. But now she's got her big eyes on me and she's running toward us. She stumbles on the grass before picking herself up, abandoning the bullhorn on the ground, and continuing on her journey. I meet her halfway and scoop her tiny body up into my arms and hold her like my life depends on it. I have to remind myself to be careful not to squish her.

"I gotta poop," she says in a baby style shouty whisper in my ear. Laughter escapes me as I revel in her innocence. I'm still not so good with the potty training stuff, so I turn to Amber and silently plead for help. My hands are so big and the kid is so small. Piper starts wiggling in my arms and making some noises that tell me it's too late. Her momma's in for a messy pull-up.

"With the next one, I'm not changing a single shitty diaper." Amber's eyes are narrowed but her tone holds no venom as she takes Piper from me. Shaking off the lingering smell of baby poop, I search for Zander who is now standing by himself near a tree off to the side of the cluster of people at the swings. His eyes are distant as he watches our family of misfits, felons, and killers gathering around the next generation of Forsaken.

My brothers smile at one another, their old ladies, and their kids in a way I haven't seen in a damn long time. Their old ladies seem to be relaxed for the first time in almost two years. Their kids rush around and play recklessly, yelling loudly, letting all of the pure joy of childhood burst out of them. Everything we do, all the illegal shit, and all the violence that we endure because of it—it's all fucking worth it in this moment. Watching these kids be kids and feel safe and protected. Knowing their daddies and mommies will lay down their lives to keep them safe.

From the middle of the crowd, Chey waves at Zander, trying to bring him into the fold. He shrugs her off, but her smile never fades. She says something to Holly—a woman she's not known very long, but is still her mother in every way that matters—and the kid looks whole. She always looked like she was missing something until Holly came along.

Fuck. Fatherhood is turning me into some kind of ginormous pussy.

I pass Chel on my way to Z and place a kiss on top of her head. She smiles up at me the way she always has—like a sister to a brother—because that's what we are to one another. Hate seeing this woman drop to her knees and take dick for no reason, but nothing I can say or do stops her. Best I can do is make it damn clear to my brothers that if they hurt her, they answer to me.

"We still on for Tuesday?" I ask. She shoots me a smile and confirms that she's not ditching my ass, nor has she ratted me out to her sister. I tell her she's a good woman and continue on toward my son.

When I reach Zander, I nudge his shoulder with my elbow and nod my head at the crowd. In the center, Stephen and Izzy—Chief's kids—are dancing around with their older, half-sister, Elle, cheering them on. Even Xavier, Chel's son, is dancing along. Elle's doing her best to ignore the kid exists. Nic jumps in with them, Robin in her arms, and she dances like a damn fool herself. Duke smiles on from the sidelines before he grabs Alex and drags her into the crowd of lunatics dancing around to no music. I catch sight of Jim as he clasps Ryan on the shoulder. The father-son duo share a rare smile before Ruby pulls Ryan into the dancing crowd and Jim heads off to his truck where he turns on a classic rock station and blares it. I turn away to see Ryan standing in the happy crowd, with a scowl on his face, still not moving. He keeps shaking his head at his mother, but she doesn't give up.

"A pretty girl asks you to dance, you don't turn her down, son."

"It's weird," Zander says quietly. I barely hear him over the music. "They all like each other."

"We're a family," I say. I don't address the fact that not all my brothers get along very well. Getting along and liking eachother is nothing compared to the bond and loyalty we all have for eachother and our patch. I don't have to like these assholes to love them.

"Mom and I didn't do much stuff with the club back home," he says. I've been waiting for my boy to talk to me for months now. He'll talk about anything and everything except what his life was like before I came along. It's never set well with me, but I tried to push and it only ended in a fight. "The guys would come by the house to fix the sink or something. Maybe even to yell at me when mom yelling didn't do any good, but it was never like this."

"I'm sorry." The words feel like they should be easy to say, but they're not. He shrugs them off regardless. "You never should have wondered about your dad."

"I didn't. Mom always talked about you. Sometimes it would make her cry, but she wanted me to know I had a dad. We should have been here. She kept you from us."

"No," I say firmly. "Son, I wasn't a good man. Your mom left me so she could protect you and give you a little slice of normal. You don't have to like every choice she makes, but she's your mom. The shit she does is *always* to protect you."

"It didn't work," he says sardonically. "Other moms bake cookies and shit. My mom cleans her guns for fun. My friends' parents stopped letting them come over to the house because the woman is crazy."

Amber's teaching me to pick and choose my battles, so I don't tell him not to swear. Not that I give a fuck. It's just a word, but Holly's had complaints from two of his teachers about his language. I almost marched down to that school and told them to pull the sticks out of their fucking twats. Probably wouldn't help the boy make friends though.

"Yeah, but she's crazy hot when she gets going." My voice is wistful which makes the boy cringe and me laugh.

"No, I mean like one time the bus driver didn't make sure I got off at the right stop and he didn't know where I was when mom called the school. Mom kept yelling that she was going to gut the dude if he got me lost again. Another time some kid's mom wanted me to apologize to her kid after he pushed me, so I decked his ass. Mom didn't like that much either."

Zander—*my son*—doesn't look at me as he speaks. He just continues with his story about Amber. He calls her mom—as he should—like it's the most natural thing in the world while I sit here and can't even fucking breathe because he's here and he's real and he's mine. And he's talking to me. He calls her mom all the time, but he doesn't fucking talk to me, so it hits me extra hard this time.

"What'd your mom do?" I ask. I already know she went crazy on the bitch just from the way Z says the woman talked to her, but I like hearing his voice. I'm starting to figure out what his voice sounds like when he gets excited or when he's angry but refuses to show it. This tone though, it's sad which kills me.

"Mom showed the lady her Forsaken tattoo and told her it means that she belongs to Wyatt Strand and even though the lady doesn't know what that means now, she better pray she never has to find out. That's the first time I really remember hearing her saying your name."

And I'm gutted.

CHAPTER TWENTY-ONE

Amber

April 2016

Mancuso's downfall

"Again," I shout. Alex's eyes flutter, surprise evident on her face. I've scared her. She needs to toughen up. She circles me in a fighter's stance and takes a swing at me that I easily block. What she lacks in physical abilities she more than makes up for with her stubbornness. She's young, but she's got a lot of heart, and despite the fact that she can't throw a punch to save her goddamn life, I think I like her.

Ruby heard from Gloria, Alex's aunt on her father's side, a few weeks ago that Carlo should be released soon. I don't know what kind of deal they have, but Gloria made a call to the boys right after, acting like she never spoke to Ruby. All Ruby said when I asked her about it was, "Boys will be boys. Even as men, they need a mother's supervision."

According to Gloria, the feds are delaying Carlo's release for as long as they can, still trying to rack up charges against him and his known associates. Nobody's talking, and that's a good thing. If the feds lock down Mancuso with RICO, they're one step closer to targeting Forsaken. Nobody seems worried about RICO. Right now, we're all just focused on staying alive.

Wyatt won't talk about the plans for New York except to tell me that he's got everything under control. I thought we'd made progress after Forsaken locked down the Petrov family as allies, but I guess we haven't. So much has happened since he promised I could come to New York with the club. After Ian and Mindy's wedding he told me he wants me to have his last name. It's not the first time we've talked about making it legal, but it's the first time I think we might be solid enough to actually get there. He even said "after New York", he'd make it happen. Then, when Nic was voted in and again when Jeremy was patched, he said the same thing—"after New York".

I've been hearing it for months. *After New York.* I can feel it coming—the trip back East. The tension in the air is palatable. Wyatt told me the boys agreed to letting me, Ruby, Alex, and Mindy go with them. Elle is going to remain in town and oversee our intel on our way out there. With Holly pregnant and Nic with a new baby, neither one is interested in arguing about staying behind. Chey didn't even ask if she could go, and that's a damn good thing. The girl is barely legal. Jeremy asked the club to vote her in the day he was patched—a move reminiscent of my old man—but she's still Fort Bragg's VP's daughter first and foremost. Hell, even I would have lost my shit over letting her go.

We've been making all these plans, prepping for the trip, but something feels off. In my gut, I know the guys don't plan on bringing us. It's going to get ugly, but Ruby and I talked about it. We're going. Come Hell or high water, we're not letting our men ride into battle without us.

"I'm wiped," I tell Alex truthfully. She stops bobbing around me and wonders off. She finds Ryan perched on a bar stool and climbs onto his lap. He holds her with a gentleness that I don't think anybody would have ever expected from him. Christ, even when he was a kid I wanted to drown his ass in a shallow pool. She's only there for a minute before Duke gives Ryan a hand wave. I focus my attention on the men in the room as they quietly head down the hall toward the chapel.

From behind the bar, Mishy stares at me wide-eyed. She nods her head to signal me over. I follow her lead to the side room with the pool table in it. She leans against the table, eyes the room, and then levels her gaze on me.

"Boys got a call," she says quietly, so casual that it's like we're talking about taking the kids to the park or some shit. It's not casual though. As far as I know, my sister's made it a point to keep her nose out of club business. It just never ends well. Just one more thing we don't see eye to eye on. "Mancuso's being released within the next week. His lawyer says he should have been out by now, but paperwork keeps getting lost. They think it's the feds fucking things up on purpose."

"Wouldn't doubt it." I try to keep my voice low, but it's hard. With the boys out of the room, it's so quiet in here. The kids are all having a play date with Wyatt and

Grady's moms. It's weird being so kid-free, even if it is just for an afternoon.

"Another thing. They're not bringing you with them. I was cleaning out behind the bar and overheard Ryan and Ian arguing about it." My hackles rise at her words. I fucking hate having it confirmed. They never planned on bringing us along. Not even for a moment. "Ryan said Alex has this plan to offer herself up to her dad, but he won't let her do it. Ian thinks it's a good plan. He wants you all with them, but he was out-voted."

"Goddamn it. I knew they'd try and pull this shit." My words are a shout and they draw attention. Ruby heads over, followed by Mindy, Holly, and Alex who trail behind. Nic stays at the bar, perched on a bar stool. For the first time in months, she doesn't have her daughter attached to her hip. Elle, who was at one of the tables in the main room, abandons the laptop she's been working on and joins the crowd, albeit at a distance.

"There's more," Mishy whispers. She leans in and sighs, nervously eyeing our audience. I give Ruby a nod to which she gets the other women to take a few steps back. They all stand around awkwardly, giving us our space but not really retreating.

"Tell me," I say, encouragingly. She sighs and takes several shaky breaths. Whatever she has to say can't be good. My own sister won't meet my eyes.

"They reached out to Detroit for back-up, just like they did when they went and got Alex. The club put Davey in charge. He's bad news and after all the shit with Rig—they just can't trust Detroit, okay?"

Not much rattles Michele Wallace, so when she's freaking out, it automatically freaks me out too. The past few months have been good for us, helped us to establish that sisterly bond that's been missing for years. I finally got to meet my nephew, who is cool as hell. And she's gotten to know my kids, too. Zander figured out pretty quickly that Mishy's a lost girl, and that wasn't a fun conversation, but they've gotten to know each other well enough that I don't think it matters to him anymore.

"Davey's shady, but Rig's gone. I made sure of that."

"I don't want to get into it," she says. "Not here. Just, please. Tell the boys they can't trust Davey."

"Sis, that's not gonna fly. I can't run my man's shit like that without telling him why."

Mishy leans in closer, her eyes glassy with unshed tears.

"I know what Rig did to you. He did the same thing to me and when he was done, he passed me off to Davey. Rig was a cakewalk by comparison. There's worse shit they've done. I can't prove any of it and all it'd do is open old wounds. What I've already said is enough. Don't let our guys trust Detroit."

"How did you know?" I've never talked to anyone about that. Not really anyway. The only person who could have any idea is Torque. My eyes fall closed as I try to regulate my breathing long enough to compose myself. Torque, Mishy, and I all grew up together. His dad was a brother in Detroit. Torque was patched in there and only transferred after some shit went down between he and Rig a few years ago. As he was leaving he was really insistent to make sure I was okay. He kept asking if I was scared or if anything was bothering me. No matter how many times I told him I was fine, he didn't believe me.

"Doesn't matter," she says. People give her crap for what she does, but my sister is loyal. I want to tell her I'm sorry and that this is one thing I never wanted to share. I want to ask her about the secrets she can't prove and everything else, but we have an audience close by and we weren't raised to apologize for shit we didn't do. I have a role here and it's not to wipe her tears. She came to me for help, not comfort. Instead of throwing my arms around my sister and selfishly crying about our damage, I turn to the women, idly waiting for us to do something.

"What's going on?" Ruby asks.

"The guys are going rogue. They don't plan on bringing us with them. They want to enlist Detroit's help, but we have it on good authority that's a bad idea," I say, just loud enough for them all to hear me. In the back, Elle shakes her head and weaves her way to the front.

"And we're making this decision based on what intel?" Of course Elle takes issue with this. Her entire role here is intel and keeping the authorities as far away from the club as possible while this plays out.

Now's not the time for my sister and best friend to sort out their issues. They share a man, even if Elle won't acknowledge it. Diesel may be Elle's old man, but he's my nephew's uncle. Neither Diesel nor Mishy talk about Xavier's father. They don't need to. After the way that piece of shit treated my sister, I know damn well he's no longer breathing. If I had known the way it really was for her back then, I'd have been a better sister. I wouldn't have abandoned her the way I did. I could have stuck by her side and pulled her out of that hell myself. At the end of the day, I'm just grateful that she had somebody. Now, my only hope with that situation is that Elle can come to terms with the fact that Mishy isn't going anywhere.

"It's solid intel," Mishy says, her eyes free of judgment as she stares at Elle. I don't blame Elle for taking issue with her late father's affair with my sister, but damn if the woman can't hold a grudge.

"I didn't ask for you opinion, bitch."

"And I didn't ask for yours," Mishy retorts.

"Well, nobody asked for yours either." Now it's Holly butting in, her eyes narrowed on Elle. I can barely make sense of what the actual hell is happening right now.

"Do we have a problem?"

"We're about to," Mindy says in a deadly cool manner. Ian's wife is gorgeous. Beautiful blonde hair, bright, glowing eyes. She's got a great figure and she's kind as hell—when she wants to be—but the woman is as twisted as her husband. She slides up to Holly, standing protectively over her cousin.

"I can defend myself," Holly gripes to Mindy.

"What is your problem lately?" Nic shouts at Holly from the bar stool she refuses to abandon.

"Okay, enough!" Ruby shouts. I probably should have shut it down sooner, but truth be told, I was kind of enjoying myself. There's too much history and trauma here for these bitches to keep playing nice when just below the surface, we're all about to fall apart. "You're grown ass women, not little fucking girls, so start acting like it. You can pull each other's hair out later. Right now, we have shit to take care of."

"We've talked about this. They're going to get themselves killed if they go alone," Mindy says, staring at her mother-in-law with sorrow filling her eyes. "They need the numbers we can provide. They need to rest easy knowing people they can trust have their backs. Even if those people have pussies."

"I know, baby," Ruby says softly.

"What the hell are we going to do?" I say with wide eyes, staring at Ruby.

I almost miss Alex backing up, her sweaty, exhausted body lumbering toward the hall. She throws her arms up in the air and shouts, "Don't give them a choice."

And with that, she turns around and hauls ass down the hall toward the chapel. All I can think is "oh shit" as I chase after her. Ruby and Mindy are on my heels, the three of us fighting to get to Alex first, but it's too late. By the time we round the corner to the hallway, she's already kicking at the solid wood French doors to the chapel.

CHAPTER TWENTY-TWO

Alex

I'm not thinking clearly. Okay, I'm not thinking at all. I just react, and once my feet are in motion, I can't seem to stop myself. This club, this family—they've turned me into someone the old me wouldn't recognize.

And I love her.

The old Alexandra Mancuso would never dream of barging in on a meeting among men. She was too timid, too scared. But that was before a group of unruly bikers showed up and whisked me away to a life I never dreamed possible. That was before she had to find a way to forgive her brother for the unforgivable. That was before men died and women were hurt in a war that began all because of a promise a man made to a woman years ago. And my big mouth is what lit the match.

The new Alexandra Mancuso isn't afraid to be rude when she needs to. No, she does what she has to in order to protect her family.

All of her family, and that includes the thick-headed idiots who think they can take on the Italian mafia without backup they can trust. It means being the bad guy when the rest of the club's women are trying to manipulate their way into getting what they want. It means loving a family enough to refuse to let them get themselves hurt.

The double wooden doors fly open before I can kick through them. I jump back at what meets me on the other side. Grady, Ryan, Ian, Duke, and Diesel all stand in front of Wyatt, the club's new president, with their guns trained on me. Even Michael and Leo are in the background, behind the rest of the club, with their gold Desert Eagles in hand. Only Torque is missing.

The men are not supposed to take their pieces into Church, but this isn't Church. If it were, they wouldn't have two Mafiosos in there with them. They weren't talking business. They were sitting in there figuring out how to slip past their women without us noticing. So I don't cower. Two years ago I would've flipped out and needed a week to recover. But not now. Ryan taught me that. Don't cower. Men smell weakness and they prey upon it. I just hope he knows what he's done.

"What the fuck, babe?" Ryan shouts at me, his expression livid. I ignore the rest of their fuming faces and focus on my man. Slowly, they all lower their guns and start shouting at once. Less than a minute passes before I'm joined by the rest of the women. They chased me down the hall, likely trying to stop what I just did. They were fast, but I've spent my entire life running from things I fear, so I'm faster.

"Shut up!" Amber screams from my right. She's only a few inches taller than me, but her presence is mighty. Amber Wallace was born a princess in this world, much like I was in my old world, but nobody ever tried to extinguish her blaze. They nurtured it, gave her a voice, showed her how to be strong, and they demanded she be fierce in everything. That's what Forsaken women are—they're fierce.

No, *we're* fierce.

They don't have to vote me in and give me a tattoo for me to be one of them. I'd like to see them get rid of me now.

Wyatt points his finger at Amber and warns her that she's going to pay for this show of insolence later, to which she smirks and blows him a kiss, telling him she can't wait. Duke's the first to break. He shakes his head, turns on his heel, screams, "Fuck," and stomps back into the room. Slowly, the rest of the men follow.

"We have something to say." I do my best to keep my voice steady, but it breaks at the end when Ryan moves toward me. Hurt fills his eyes, both for what I'm doing and what he's doing to me, no doubt. I put my hand up to stop him and shake my head. I won't lean on him for this. I made the choice to interrupt the boys on my own, and I'll answer for that choice on my own.

"No shit?" Grady says. A tone of snide disapproval evident in his tone. Holly moves through the room and moves to stand beside him. In a move that looks loving and supportive, she laces her fingers in his. Only, I don't miss the way her nails dig into his skin. I've come to love Holly for her quiet but firm strength. Not even Grady, the new VP, calls attention to it. His jaw ticks as he stares me down.

"You don't have to like me or trust me to listen to me," I say, my eyes still affixed to Grady's. He's been the most difficult to win over. Even Ian, my own brother, was less challenging to get to know, and that man is like Fort Knox with his heart, but I'm sneaky. I've wormed my way in. He just won't admit it yet.

"This isn't about *liking* the choices we have to make. This is about doing the things we must in order to protect our family."

"You're not going," Ryan says tersely.

"And how are you going to stop me?" I ask with ice in my voice.

"I'll tie you to a chair if I have to," he says.

Feeling brave, I flit my eyes to my twin brother and smile. Michael and I barely look alike now, thanks to puberty. Ian watches us, his half siblings, with deft interest.

"You wanna tell him how well that's going to work, or shall I?"

Ryan's eyes slide to Michael, dislike still as evident as ever. I don't realize what I've said until it's out there. Michael, in a fit of rage, tied me to a chair and beat me in an attempt to save my life. It was wrong, and after nearly two years of healing, I've forgiven him. Ryan hasn't, and I'm not sure if I were in his shoes I'd forgive him either. He doesn't know Michael the way I do. He doesn't know how we were raised, the way our father sees women, or the way he thinks they ought to be punished for stepping out of line. They really need to get over this shit at some point, though. I might hit menopause before my man lets go of the grudge at this rate.

My mom, Ruby, was Queen Bee around here for over fifteen years when my stepdad, Jim, gave up his presidency. It's only been a few months, but they're happier this way. The transition has been pretty smooth, all things considered. The biggest obstacle has been Ryan holding an officer position as sergeant-at-arms while Jim no longer has a rank. His choice, though. Wyatt tried to at least make him his VP, but Jim's maintained that he wants easy from now on. Jim wanting easy explains why he stands in the corner, silent and not meeting anyone's eyes. I notice that Mom is watching him closely.

"Enough," she says loudly. Even Ryan simmers down a little at her voice. It's still weird, thinking about the fact that, for all intents and purposes, she's his mom, too. I share her blood, but she raised him. Neither of us is any less her child, but it sure makes thinking about the whole situation strange.

"In the last two years I've seen this club run itself into the ground because we're making decisions with our hearts and not our heads. Part of that is on me. I'll never be able to repay you all for what you've done to save my daughter," she pauses and looks at Michael. "And now my son, too."

I don't cry much anymore, but if ever there was something that could make it happen...

"I know why you want to protect us, but you need to look around." Her voice is softer now. She's pleading. Mom and I have talked about this a lot on our own, a little with Mindy, and even some with Jim. Jim's old school through and through, and even though he gave up his spot as president because he was going soft, he's still rougher around the edges than the rest of them. As long as it's not his call, he's good with letting us come. It's a weird paradox he's got going on in his head, and I don't pretend to understand it. I wouldn't want to have to make the calls he's had to.

"Every single one of your women has blood on her hands on behalf of this club."

"Not putting you in danger, Ma," Ian says, finally breaking the quiet.

"You're my child, baby. You don't get to put me in a position outlive you. I won't do it."

"You're walking a thin line, woman," Wyatt says with his eyes boring holes into Amber's head.

"Lied to me," she says. "Seems you're walking that same line yourself."

There's a venom in his voice that makes me grateful it's not directed at me when he asks who's going to watch their kids. The ice in his voice chips away at my tough exterior. I've badassed enough for the day. I'm basically done now.

It's not Wyatt's size that unnerves me—it's just him. He's never been anything but decent toward me, but underneath all the decency lies something disturbing that makes me wary.

"Your mom, my dad," she says. He opens his mouth and starts telling her he's not going to risk the mother of his children while she yells back with every bit as much anger and intensity in her voice. It starts out as one general insult after another before sliding into something deeper than I think any of us are prepared for.

"I made a promise to our son that I would bring him to his dad. The only thing that boy wanted after Rig had a gun to his head was to see you. The only thing that let him sleep at night after he had to watch his mom kill a man not two feet from him was knowing he was finally going to get to know *you.* And now you want to run off and risk your life, risk hurting our boy more? No. If you think I'm doing *anything* to take you away from him, you are dead fucking wrong."

I knew about this. Ryan told me one night while we were lying in bed. Hearing it in bed, being told by someone else is one thing. Standing here, hearing it from the person who experienced, it is quite another.

"Either you take us with you and use us the way you're supposed to, or you're signing your own death warrants. This plan you have is half-assed. Now, are you boys going to listen to what we have to say, or do we need to wait until you leave so we can follow?"

The silence drones on, so long that I practically break out in hives while I wait for somebody to break. Ryan's eyes lock on mine from across the room. With a small nod, I welcome him over, and he envelopes me in his arms. I don't realize how much I need his comfort until he's wrapped around me.

Ryan bends and whispers in my ear, "I don't like this."

"You promised," I say. "We don't want to be going back on our promises, now do we?"

"Sometimes I want to go back to when the only thing that mattered was my bike and strange pussy," he says grouchily. "Fuck lot less complicated."

"Fuck lot less meaningful," I respond. He holds me tighter, and it's in this moment that I know I've won. I want to protect my man, and he wants to protect me, but he also wants to marry me. He wants babies with me. And I want all those things, too, even if not right this minute. I want us more than anything, but I *need* him to let me make my own choices. He doesn't like it, and he doesn't have to, but if he wants this legal and he wants our children, he's going to deal with it. And he knows it. For the first time in my life, I feel on even keel with a man. He wants me as much as I want him, and that means something.

More than something.

Eventually Grady concedes. He stares right at me, waiting for me to speak. Still not happy with me. And I wonder if ever there will be a day that he looks at me with something other than disgust.

"From the beginning, all my father has wanted is to have me and Michael back. So we set up an exchange. Let him think we're going in, giving him what he wants. This war has taken too many lives, fractured too many relationships. Let him think he's won. Even if he doesn't believe it, he wants his protégé back. He'll risk it for Michael."

"She's right," Michael says. "If he thinks Leo and I are still loyal, he'll want us back. He'll want Al back just to prove he can take her."

"This plan is a lot more controlled, fewer surprise factors, and less likely to get you all killed than what you were planning to do on your own."

"I don't like it," Jim says from the corner. "As a father, I hate it, and I sure as hell don't want my wife there. But it's smart." Jim meets my eyes from where he stands, now with Mom by his side. He smiles softly, almost sadly, and nods his head as if to tell me I did good.

From behind me, heavy footsteps fall against the concrete floor, but I don't turn around. It's only when Jeremy pushes his way through the men—his brothers—until he's standing, open-mouthed, staring past us that the footsteps come to a halt. I turn around to see what Jeremy's looking at and gasp. Standing in the hall, behind us women—women who have now turned around to stare in collective astonishment—is Butch Whelan. His long grayish-black hair is tied back in a man bun, the wrinkles that line his face a testament to the life he's lived. The glow in his eyes is unmistakable.

To my right, Nic is frozen in place. Her eyes are wide and filled with tears as she stares up at her father. Behind her is Duke, his hands on her shoulders.

"Still want to go with us, or would you rather stay home with this old bastard?" Duke's love for my friend warms my heart. It takes me longer than it should to realize that he planned this. I don't know how he could since Butch has been in prison the last several years, but somehow he did. And Butch is here. It's smart—giving his old lady the one thing she wants in order to keep her home. It wouldn't keep me home, but my father's never looked at me the way Butch is looking at Nic.

"You gonna stand there and cry, baby girl, or you gonna give your old man a hug?" Half a second later, Nic throws herself into his arms. Butch raises his head and smiles at Jeremy, who still hasn't moved.

"Cut looks good on you, son," Butch says. Jeremy juts his chin out and nods, doing his best not to embarrass himself in front of his brothers. As the newest patched member of Forsaken, he's got a lot to prove still. Only when Grady moves behind Jeremy and whispers in his ear saying, "You're never too much of a man to love your father," does Jeremy actually move. He runs full speed ahead at his dad and slams into the older man with a force that nearly knocks them all over. But the once-broken, now-whole family hangs tight.

"Where's my grandbaby?" Butch asks, leveling a gaze at Duke. He then turns his attention to Jeremy. "And where's Miss Priss? You asked her yet?"

Jeremy clears his throat and rubs the back of his neck as the hug breaks up. He avoids Grady's glare. Finally, Mom breaks up the tension with her laughter, saying, "You always did have a big mouth, Butch. Welcome home, honey."

CHAPTER TWENTY-THREE

Wyatt—

"You look like shit," Mary says. Mary Wallace, affectionately known as Bloody Mary, peers up at me from her small, hunched over frame. She's got wrinkles on top of wrinkles, and she's unsteady on her feet. Amber says she has a cane she's supposed to use, but the moment I asked if she needed it, she informed me the only thing she'd need it for was to shove it up my ass. The family resemblance between the Wallace women does not go unnoticed.

"I feel like shit," I admit. Not only am I tired, but my heart is sore. Leaving the kids this morning was hard as fuck. Zander understood why we were leaving, what we're doing. But Amber's speech about what went down with Rig still bothers me. I don't know if it'll ever not bother me.

I tried to focus on the road and the shit we've got going on with Mancuso the best I could. After we got the call that the fucking prick had been released two days ago, we made the call to Emilio, his underboss, about setting up the exchange. I played it as even as I could, telling Emilio that "the little bitch isn't worth it" regarding Alex.

She winced when I said the words but took it in stride. Then we all scattered, took care of our shit, and met back up on the edge of town to ride out together. Just like last time, we have some men on bikes and some in the van. Only this time, I have my crazy-ass woman on the back.

We rode for ten hours with only the necessary stops to get here—to the middle of bumfuck Nevada. To the random passerby, we're at the West Wendover Rustic Motel. Not that anyone just passing through would see the sign or the dilapidated buildings that make up the former motel. We're miles off the road, stretched out in the middle of a nothing desert without so much as a grocery store for miles. I've always considered this place a weird juxtaposition. This is our Mother Charter—it's a holy land of sorts for Forsaken.

The club's founding members are all from Detroit, and they spent the majority of their lives in the Motor City while their kids were growing up and they were working. This place was always special for Clutch, Amber's granddad, though. After coming back from war, he holed up here, at this motel, for a few months before Mary hunted him down and brought him home. It was out here in the desert, with nothing for miles around, that Clutch found a way to live in a world he no longer understood. Some of the younger guys don't know the history—they never bothered to check it out. One of the first things Amber's dad, Thumper, ever said to me—after he said, "Touch my daughter and I'll fucking kill you"—was to impart Forsaken's history on me. It was important to him—still is—that people understand why we exist. We were founded on the philosophy that no man should have to adhere to a government they don't believe in. No man should be forced to kill for any cause but his own. Forsaken makes our own laws. We don't force others to live our way, and won't be forced into living theirs. We exist outside the social structure that makes others feel safe. Because only outside of that safety net are we free.

"You didn't bring my babies," Mary chides. I reach down and brush my thumb against her cheek. She narrows her worn eyes and bites back a smile.

"Next time," I promise.

"You flirting with my man?" Amber says teasingly, over my shoulder. She walks up and kisses Mary on her head. They had their reunion earlier, but they've always been close. I like seeing them together. Being around all these old farts gives me hope that we might live long enough to be that old and wrinkly.

"You can call him yours when you have his ring on your finger."

I give Mary a look that tells the old broad to shut the hell up, but it does no good. One of the few people Chel keeps in contact with regularly is her grandma. Mary always said that all women take dick for protection. It's just a question of whether or not she's treated like a whore just in the bedroom or on the street as well. So when Mary gets going on this ring business, I know damn well why.

"I have his tattoo on my back and his two babies," Amber says snidely. "That's enough."

I pull her against me.

"I'm tired, Mary. Gonna hit the sack."

Mary waves us off. As we move away from the cabin, I catch sight of Alex and Ryan standing by Rage's cabin, talking to him. Rage, Ryan's grandfather and Jim's father, reaches out and pulls Alex toward him. He places a kiss on her cheek. Well, shit. The crazy little bitch won over Rage.

"Where are you at with that?" Amber says, nodding toward Alex. She's not asking if I approve of her or her relationship with Ryan. She wants to know if we plan on voting her in.

"Giving it time. Once shit settles, gonna talk to Trigger about it." Ryan came to me right after I took the gavel to see if getting Alex voted in was ever going to happen. I told him basically the same thing—that once we get past this war with Mancuso, we can revisit the idea. The last thing we need is tension among the brothers, though I'm not sure there would be any anymore. Still, it's not worth it.

"Good. She's young and a little soft around the edges, but Ryan could use soft. I like her."

"Of course you do," I say and pull her into the cabin Clutch told us we could have for the night. Our cabin is toward the back of the property, one of the better-shielded buildings. Our cabin is also in better condition than most of them. The water runs fairly evenly, and the small window unit actually heats the place up reasonably well. I'd have given it to another couple, but I won't question my elders. I'm a charter president, and that demands respect, so I let it go. Besides, I want my woman as warm and comfortable as can be. Even if I am still annoyed with her over that shit she and the other women pulled at the clubhouse.

"It's been years since I've spent that long on a bike," she says as she yawns and plops down on the bed.

"You too tired to fuck?"

"Nah, but don't expect any special moves."

I move toward her, shoving my hand in my jeans pocket. This little bastard has been burning a hole in my pocket the entire ride. I've had it for months but wanted to wait until Mancuso was taken out. Now, though, this feels like the right time. Regardless of what happens in the next few days, I want my woman knowing where I stand. We might not be in that crazed, early stages of falling in love anymore, but what we have is way better than that. I'm completely myself around this maddening woman. She doesn't try to show me what she thinks I want, not that I think she ever did. Amber is the same in many ways as she always has been with one exception—she's more now. Fiercer, brighter, more beautiful. Stronger, louder, more vulnerable. She's everything I ever wanted in a woman, even when she pisses me off. And if I weren't so goddamn tired and sore and worried about the coming days, I might tell her this shit.

But I don't.

Instead, I just climb into the bed next to her, shrugging off my cut and boots, dropping my jeans, and taking off my shirt. The only things I don't rid myself of are my boxers and the diamond ring in my hand.

My eyes are glued to her as I watch her strip down to her underwear. She lies back down beside me and smiles teasingly.

"I'm not going to do everything for you."

"You do enough," I say. "I can handle your panties, but don't blame me if I destroy them in the process."

Amber pulls my face to hers, peppering me with gentle kisses. On the corner of my mouth and on my nose. Another to my brow and one to the corner of my eye. We're both exhausted, but neither of us are in a hurry. I run my hands up and down her curves, loving every bit of flesh I'm fucking lucky enough to touch.

"Thank you for this, bringing us. I know you didn't want to, but we deserve to be here." Amber's voice is soft, a far cry from the harsh tone she took me with earlier in the chapel. Or was it yesterday? Every bit of me is so fucking exhausted that I can't tell anymore. I press my lips to her cheek and trail kisses down her neck to her tits. She's always had great tits. They're larger now, hang a little lower than before, but they're still perfect. I missed out on her body after having a baby—both times—and that's never not going to eat me alive.

"Mishy and I talked. You can't trust Davey, just like you couldn't trust Rig. They're not good men," she says slowly. I stare up at her and pin her to me.

"You say what you gotta say, baby. I'm here." She's trying to tell me something, but I don't know what just yet.

"They used my sister. They broke her. What Rig did to her is worse than what he did to me." Her voice is shaky now. The sorrow in her eyes breaks me as I try to wrap my mind around what she's telling me. She places a finger over my lips and shakes her head. "We can deal with that history later. What I'm saying right now is that you need us. You can't trust anybody is going to fight as hard for your life as I will. Me and your brothers...we're it, baby. And I know you don't want me here. I know you want me at home, nice and safe with our babies, but that's not the woman you picked. You picked me because I can set your shit straight even when you can't."

"You shouldn't have to live like this. All the violence and death. I'm sorry, baby. I want better for you, but I'm too selfish to let you go."

"I was born into this. I chose this. Taking Rig out wasn't even hard. It was easy. He threatened our son. I didn't think twice. I just filled him with enough bullets to make sure he'd never take another breath. And for a brief moment, I liked the rush of it. I liked the power I had, being able to stop him. So you tell me, what am I supposed to do with that? How do I live inside the law, knowing I can end a man's life if I want to? Knowing how it feels to watch a man die? How do I live normal when I have that coursing through me?"

Giving her a sad smile, I run my hands up and down her side before slowly peeling her panties off of her. I shrug out of my boxers and hover over her. A soft kiss to her lips and then one to her chest. I lick and suck at her nipples before moving lower. I keep my movements as slow as possible, almost painfully so, as I part her thighs and waste no time in dragging my tongue over her pussy. She grows wet with my attention. Lick.

Kiss. Nibble. When she's good and ready, I focus my attention on her clit. First with my tongue and, when she bucks against me and moans loudly, I wrap my lips around it and suck. She's so wet and ready, her pussy throbbing for me. My dick is so fucking hard that I can barely think. Just before my woman explodes into my mouth, I withdraw and crawl back up her body. In one fluid motion, I'm inside her. The ring is still in my hand, hidden in my closed fist. We move together, restless and needy, but patient. I don't know what's going to happen in the coming days or weeks. I don't know what life after Mancuso looks like. All we really have is right now, so I do my best to make it last.

I lather her with attention but not enough to push her over the edge. I impale her once and then slide out slowly and back in at the same leisurely pace. Sweet, sweet torture heats my body as we move. I want to tell her that I didn't want her to come because I'm afraid of what's going to happen. I'm afraid I won't make it home. I'm afraid we'll succeed and I'll have to watch a young woman witness her father's execution. I'm afraid of sending a young man into a war that ends with him taking over his family's business. A move that places him in his father's shadow and encourages the monster within. I'm afraid that when it's all settled, even when our days are normal and our nights are full of peace, that we won't recover. We'll jump at every sound. We'll destroy our enemies before we know the threat level. We'll tear ourselves apart because we no longer know how to just be—we only know how to wade through blood.

"Nothing you tell me is going to get you out of marrying me," I say. Her eyes go wide, her mouth assumes an O shape, and she grunts. She needs more. I pull a pillow over and pause my ministration to shove it under her ass. At this new angle, I can hit her deeper, giving her what she needs. My balled fist spares my thumb to rub fast, insistent circles over her swollen nub. She clamps down around my cock. A shudder runs through me. We're nearly there, close to coming. I'm pacing myself, timing her body's responses. We've done this dance enough times for me to know how it ends. When her body shakes and mine heats, my limbs tightening to the point of no return, it's time.

"Every ounce and every breath," I say, abandoning her pussy and anchoring myself with my elbows beside her head. I take her hands in mine, holding her in place. With all the focus I can manage without losing my rhythm, I get the ring out of my palm and slide it over her left ring finger. She explodes around my cock as her hands grab onto my fists.

"Yes," she moans. Her eyes are closed, and part of me isn't totally sure if she's agreeing to marry me or if my cock is just that good. But then she mumbles, "Finally," and comes down from her high with her body shaking slightly.

"You haven't even seen the ring yet," I say, a chuckle creeping up from my throat.

"It's just jewelry, baby," she says, opening her eyes and smiling at me. I let go of her hands, and she reaches out, wrapping them around my neck. Her eyes are focused, but I don't miss how they subtly slide over to her left hand to check out the diamond Mishy picked out. My woman's smile breaks out into a grin. "I think you might have just earned yourself baby number four."

"Fuck yes, I have." A thrill runs through me, knowing that even if we do end up all fucked-up, we still have our family, and that will always make everything okay.

CHAPTER TWENTY-FOUR

Amber

My hands shake as I wrap them tighter around my man's solid frame. My right hand clutching my .22 caliber underneath the leather of his cut. Wyatt didn't like it, insisting that the pieces strapped to my body were enough, but I wouldn't have it. Anyone tries to take a shot while we're en route, I want to be ready. The five seconds it'll take to get to my other guns could be the difference between life and death. And I meant what I said when I told my man that nothing and nobody is going to stop me from bringing him back to our kids alive.

The cool April wind blows around us, my man's Harley roaring as we fly down the highway to the meet. There's some kind of vulnerability with rolling up in such a powerful machine, so exposed to the elements. Despite the helmets on our heads and the Kevlar over our hearts, we're like sitting ducks. Well-armed ducks that are ready to shed blood for what we believe in, but ducks nonetheless. I was so focused on the fact that the boys gave in to letting us come that I never thought to ask where we would be meeting Mancuso for the exchange. It's not really an exchange, though. Alex may share Carlo's last name, but she's one of us now. And Forsaken doesn't sacrifice family. Not ever.

Wyatt pulls the bike off the highway and leads us through a commercial area that gives way to abandoned commercial projects and to a dilapidated field. Shielded by two empty and decaying apartment buildings, we come to a stop. Everyone moves around quickly, fixing shit and adjusting themselves on their bikes. From the corner of my eye, I see Mindy on the back of Ian's bike. She slides a small Swiss Army knife into the crushed bun atop her head and then puts her helmet back on. The knife itself isn't big enough to kill, but it'll maim enough to save her life if it comes down to it. Ruby does the same. Alex hops off Ryan's bike and rushes over to the van where she retrieves a black drawstring bag. It looks like one of those things new sheet sets come in. She says something to Ryan to which he nods, and before she can run back to the van, dressed in all black from head to toe, he pulls her to him and kisses her like it's the last time he's ever going to be able to do so. I turn away, not liking the thought that comes to mind.

It might be.

No. We can't let it. We haven't suffered for this long, gone through this much to let her die now. *I* won't allow it. When she returns, she's in something I assume her father will deem more appropriate. Blue jeans, a soft pink sweater, and flat feminine boots make up the new outfit. God only knows how she managed it that quick, but she did. She's even already got her helmet on. When Alex climbs onto the back of Ryan's bike, she's awkward and distant. They gripe at each other for a minute as if their sweet parting never happened. And then Ryan starts up his bike and rides in large circles around us. Wyatt gets us going again, but right before we take off, out of the corner of my eye, I spot Mishy rushing out of the van and hopping on the back of Diesel's bike. Shit. Elle is going to have a fucking field day with this. That man fucking knows better than to taunt his woman by letting my sister ride bitch.

As Road Captain, Diesel revs his bike and rides past us, not stopping until he's a decent distance away. Grady and Wyatt pull up behind Diesel, taking their positions as VP and President. It isn't until we're right behind Diesel's bike that I realize what's happening. I pull my man close and smile to myself. This isn't our usual formation, but it's smart. I looks around, wondering whose idea this was.

Behind us, Jim pulls up, just off to the side, Ryan comes up center, and Ian brings his bike up on Ryan's other side. Mancuso is bound to know about Ryan and Alex's relationship, so this is good. We're guarding her until the exchange. The van rolls up behind Ryan, and the rest of the guys move into position, covering the van as well. Michael and Leo are inside where Mishy was. She decided to come at the last minute. With Dad watching Zander and Piper, she reasoned he could watch Xavier, too. I just hope the old man has what little of his sanity is left when we get home.

The bikes all roar to life, the brothers revving their engines in a show of solidarity, a battle cry even. Diesel raises his pointer finger in the air, points at the sky, swivels his wrist around twice, and then points forward. We take off like a shot, at high speeds, all careful of one another, aiming not to get too close but still remain close enough. We're like a pack, refusing to be separated, refusing to be seen as anything other than one. We ride for at least ten minutes, most of which I spend calming myself down. I need to be on point so that my family—*all of my family*—makes it out of this whole. I think about everything that's happened the last few months. I remember the first time Zander saw his father and the moment when Wyatt realized Piper is his.

I think about the first night we spent in our house and how my man gave himself to me, so fully, without fear of rejection, that it brought me to tears. I think about the ring on my finger and the joy in my heart. I focus on everything that's good and right in my life. I remember Ian's wedding and the vows he and Mindy spoke to each other. They were beautiful and honest. It was so intimate that I almost had to look away. Baring their hearts to one another in front of all of us was moving to say the least. I let myself fondly remember Nic being voted in, seeing her Forsaken tattoo for the first time. I remember the joy on her face at finally feeling at home. I let myself even think about when Jeremy was patched. The brothers kept the actual patching in private, as they always do, but when it came time for him to sew on his top rocker, we all sat around and watched.

It's a beautiful thing, seeing a man give himself over to the club that way. I've never had the privilege of seeing a man sew his patches before. It's personal for them, sacred. But with what we've been up against the last few years, and everything Jeremy's done for the club, I guess my man somehow knew that we needed this. We needed to see the boy become a man.

As I let my mind wander, all the while keeping a close eye on our surroundings, I can feel it finally settling into my gut. The resolve, the ice-cold determination to protect this band of misfits at all costs. Even if it means losing myself in the process. As an old lady, my life is supposed to be put above any of the brothers. I'm supposed to come first. But what they so often don't get is that as an old lady, I'll always put my family above myself. It's unwritten, but it's there. Anybody who's been around long enough knows it. The only way you get voted in is if the club knows, beyond a shadow of a doubt, that you'll protect the pack before the individual. And I will. So will Alex. She's already proven that, and she's proving it once again right now.

The bikes slow as we approach a short dock. There, in the center of the dock, is a trio of black sedans. All Mercedes, from the looks of it. Diesel stops at least fifteen yards from the sedans. In the distance, I can see Manhattan with its gleaming buildings and intimidating skyline. If we weren't here on business, I might enjoy exploring the island. But we are, so I stay focused. At once, the old ladies dismount from their old men's bikes and stand off to the side. The doors of the sedans open and out steps two aging men, both with olive skin and bellies that keep their presence from sending fear down my spine. Neither is in the best shape. They both look worn and tired, even in their designer suits. Neither man looks nervous, but I know better. Forsaken doesn't ride up on you like this and not spark even the smallest bit of fear.

An older woman steps out of the passenger side of the middle sedan, and she smooths her hair back. Her expression is flat, but she swallows her own saliva as a younger man, no older than Ryan or Ian, climbs out of the driver's side. He looks vaguely like the shorter man I assume is Emilio. Immediately I peg him for Tony, the little prick that turned this into a full-on war. It's satisfying, setting my eyes on the bitch that sent Michael out to kill his sister. I'm going to enjoy gutting him. The woman must be Gloria, Tony's mom and Emilio's wife. She's a friend, but she's with the enemy right now. Not her choice, I know. But still, I mentally work myself up for the possibility of having to wound her if it comes down to it. I can't ask Ruby or Jim, or Alex or Michael to do it. So I promise myself that I'll be the one to do it. It's the kind thing to do.

"It seems you're outnumbered," Jim says, walking toward the Italians.

The taller one—he must be Carlo—chuckles. He shakes his head, brings a hand to his mouth and whistles. None of the brothers, not even Jim turn to look. I turn my head, followed by the rest of the old ladies. The Italians have men perched atop the three buildings behind us. Each one is carrying something similar to an AR-15. I can't really tell from here. Leaning in to Wyatt, I tell him what I've seen. I move to take my helmet off and assume the position of keeping my back to his when he whispers, "Don't take your helmet off."

"Yes, baby."

"I see my daughter, but where about my son and my solider?" Carlo's eyes are fixed on the woman by Ryan's side. She's holding his hand tightly, and I feel for her. She didn't have to do this, but she did. I love her even more for it.

From behind me, Bear and Torque slide open the door to the van and pull out Leo and Michael. Both men have one of those fabric drawstrings on their heads, and they're handcuffed. We had to make it look like they're our prisoners, so while they might be bound, they each have a key in hand to free themselves when they need to. That and the number of guns and knives we loaded them down with could slaughter a small village should they need to.

Ruby walks toward Jim. She's removed her helmet, the only one of us to do so. Her eyes are cold, trained on Carlo. She says nothing as she stops by Ryan and argues with him, eventually forcing him to let go of the woman at his side. Ryan screams, "Fuck," loudly and kicks at the tire of his Harley before crossing his arms and moving forward to stand by Diesel. With each slow, deliberate step, Ruby looks like a woman destroyed. Walking her daughter toward the man who stole her all those years ago has to eat away at her. It doesn't matter if that's not what's really happening—it can't be easy nonetheless. With tear-filled eyes, Ruby passes Jim and keeps her eyes steady on his until she turns her head forward and comes to stand right in front of Carlo. The weight of the situation is heavy on my heart.

Showing his stupidity and lack of patience, Carlo reaches out and grabs ahold of Ruby. He looks in horror as he sees Alex take a step backwards, not wanting to be close to him. The little move provides us enough time to deal with the snipers on top of the buildings. We all draw our guns, safetys off, and dive into position like we've practiced. I face Mancuso and stomp forward with the rest of my girls. Our men spin around and fire off round after round at the men atop the buildings. They're untrained and slower than they should be for the job they've been given, because it doesn't take long for our boys to take them out. Like a kid in a fucking candy store, Jeremy's got an AK-47 in hand and he's shooting at the tops of the buildings with a twisted goddamn smile on his face. I really do like this kid.

Ruby laughs despite being in Carlo's grasp. She laughs maniacally, throwing her head forward. Carlo tries to ignore the show of insanity and pulls her closer to him, like he can bully her into submission. But I know Ruby and she doesn't let him win. She throws her head back as hard as she can, connecting with his nose. Tony and Emilio both draw their guns while Gloria backs up unnoticed. When she finally does draw a piece, she points it at the back of her husband's head. But it's too late. All hell breaks loose, and our plan goes to shit.

Carlo pulls out a knife and moves it toward Ruby's throat. The woman is fucking insane, because she doesn't blink. She just slides her eyes to the woman in front of her and nods her head. It all happens so fast—with the feminine-clad figure rushing at Carlo and being thrown aside with ease. She scampers away as Carlo glares down at her and spits out something in Italian that I don't understand.

Behind me, I can hear more men approaching and being shot down by our guys. I don't let it unsettle me that shots are being fired behind me. The shots are fewer and further between, with Mancuso's men rushing at our guys and our guys taking them to the ground. I turn to check my back only to see my man with his boot to some guy's neck. I turn away right as the guy takes a bullet to the skull. Just as I do, I see it. The plan I didn't know about, the one that was so perfectly executed I can barely believe they pulled it off without most of us not knowing. The woman who rode on the back of Diesel's bike throws her helmet off, revealing herself to be Alex. She stomps forward, her face red, with her gun raised. In a matter of seconds, both Michael and Leo are free from their shackles and drawing their guns on the men at our backs.

"I love you, Mom," she says firmly as she fires off one round after another at her father's head. She misses, but it's enough. Carlo is so struck by the turn of events that he's frozen for a moment too long. Ian and Ryan rush at him, Alex ceases fire, and Ruby scampers away. Jim descends upon Carlo and throws himself onto the man, slamming his fists into the Italian's face again and again. Duke has his gun at Emilio's head. A loud shot rings off before Emilio crumples to the ground. More shots ring out as grown men cry out in agony. I don't give myself the freedom of looking back to make sure my man is okay. Instead, I move forward, toward Gloria and the situation that nobody seems to be addressing.

Tony has his mother by the throat. Her face is purple, and he's not letting up. I rush toward them, trying to avoid the chaos around me. The woman might be in poor physical shape, but she's a scrapper and manages to fight him long enough to push him off. He dives for a gun that's on the ground. I figure it must be the one Gloria had before I lost sight of her. She's standing there defenseless, with her own fucking son raising a gun to her head. He doesn't have time, though, and I fire off a few shots that barely graze his chest and one to the leg that has to hurt like a bitch. Like the fucking pussy he is, he stumbles toward the edge of the dock and throws himself over. I stand there, in shock, as I watch him disappear into the water.

When I turn around, it's eerily quiet. There are bodies everywhere, some moving and some not. Bear is down, but the rest of our guys seem fine. I want to go check on him, but I don't have the luxury. Carlo is holding on to Alex, a large knife to her throat. His eyes are crazy, and he's dripping with sweat.

"You would let them kill your own father?" Carlo asks, his question obviously for Alex.

"No," Alex says softly. "I'll give you the same respect you gave me. I'll just turn my back while I let you die. At least I know you earned your fate."

Ian gulps as Carlo presses the knife in enough to draw blood. Alex cries out in pain, and my stomach lurches at the sound. Ryan's finger twitches on the trigger of his gun. Wyatt joins me at my side, shouting "You're not getting out of this."

"I don't plan on getting out, but I can give your *whore* something to remember me by," Carlo says with a twisted smile on his face. He pulls the knife away from his own daughter's throat and drags the blade up her face. He presses it into the side of her mouth and smirks as he drags the blade from the corner of her mouth, slowly back to her ear. My mind flashes with Ian's face and the scar he bears from a scene all too similar to this. We could shoot Carlo, but the damage is already done. Blood pours from Alex's face and down her neck as she cries out in pain. Tears push at my eyes, threatening to fall down my cheeks. I feel so helpless in this situation. Like there's something I should be able to do to stop it. If we shoot, we risk missing and losing Alex. If that happens, then everything we've lose and all we've suffered is for nothing. All the pain we've endured is for naught if Alex dies.

"Stop it, Mike," Ruby cries out, a mother's love and fear evident in her voice. Abandoning reason, she rushes toward him, but he only digs into Alex's flesh further. She's losing too much blood. She can't take much more of this. When Carlo gets to her ear, he drags the knife back over her flesh toward her eye. Ruby makes it halfway to Carlo before Jim flies into action. He shoves her out of the way at the last minute and throws himself at Carlo.

The rest follow, with Ryan pulling Alex away from the monster who created her. I'm so focused on Ryan falling to the ground, Alex in his arms, bloody and screaming out in pain, that I don't see what's happening with Carlo. Our boys got him, though.

Ryan Stone, one of the meanest assholes I've ever met, screams out, with tears falling down his face. He rips his shirt and uses the torn material in his hand to cover Alex's wound. He sobs loudly, unapologetically, as he holds the only woman aside from this mother that he's ever given a shit about in his arms, unable to make her pain go away. "I'm sorry," he chants again and again as he falls apart. Alex kicks at the ground as she helps Ryan hold the shirt over her wound. It's going to scar. The cut was way too deep. My heart hurts for her, but there's nothing I can do there.

Slowly, I approach the crowd that's gathered where Jim tackled Carlo. Men are slowly standing up and backing off. Wyatt's eyes leave the men on the ground and raise to mine. Unshed tears fill his eyes, and my stomach drops. His face contorts into something unrecognizable as he stares at me. I manage to rip my eyes away from him long enough to see what's going on.

On the ground, Jim is doubled over. He has his hand on his stomach, doing his best to cover what I can only assume is a knife wound. Dark-red liquid seeps out from beneath his fingers, covering his hand in his own blood. Michael stands to the side, holding Ruby against his chest, her head firmly shoved into his pecs. When she breaks away, she spins around and eyes her husband on the ground. Leo and Duke grab at Carlo, who is now either unconscious or dead, and pull him away. Ruby runs to Jim and pulls him up against her chest. He screams out from the movement, his shaking hand no longer able to stop the bleeding from the side of his stomach. I can't make sense of it. We're wearing bulletproof vests. That should have protected us. But judging by the way Jim's holding his wound, Carlo got him at the exact right angle and was able to get under his vest rather than through.

"Come on, baby. You're fine. You have to be fine," Ruby cries into Jim's head. She rocks back and forth, cradling him to her like a protective lioness.

Jim slowly blinks up at her, and he gives her a weak smile. He tries to laugh at her words, but he can't. His face is ashen, and even with Ruby's hand on his wound, it's still seeping blood. He smarts, saying, "Just a flesh wound, Mama."

And in that moment, we're all propelled into action. The men coordinate how best to get both Jim and Alex to a hospital. Somewhere in the back of my mind, it seeps through that nobody's worried about Bear, which means we lost him. I fight back the tears, deciding now's not the time to mourn my old man's brother. Everything moves so fast and so slow at the same time. It's like I'm watching it in a movie. I do my best to go through the motions of getting everyone moving, but the look on

Wyatt's face tells me it's more than a flesh wound. I shake my head, my eyes trained on him. Slowly, gravely, my old man nods. He's wrong. He has to be.

"No," Ian says. It feels more like a whisper, but it's loud enough for all of us to hear it. He's the only one not moving, remaining stock-still. His eyes volley between his adopted father and his half sister. He looks like he's about to be sick. "It can't end like this."

The End

CEASE (BAYONET SCARS, NO. 7)

Dear reader,

Thank you so much for taking the time to read this book. What follows Haunt is Jim and Ruby's story, which marks the culmination of a story that spans decades of pain and loss, but also extraordinary love. I hope you join me as we wrap up the *Bayonet Scars* series and bid farewell to the Forsaken Motorcycle Club. In true, JC Emery fashion, I've saved the best for last.

ACKNOWLEDGMENTS

Thank you to my mom and sisters. You three are the absolute best. To my Jewels for encouraging me every step of the way. To Danielle Sanchez for everything you do. My wonderful cover artist, Brenda Gonet at Star Bound Books, who perfectly depicted Wyatt and Amber and my amazing editor, Michele Milburn, who never loses her patience with me. Big thank you to everyone on Team JC Emery. You're all amazing. To the bloggers who kept asking where *Haunt* is, and to my readers who thought to message me demanding more Forsaken. I wish I had the time to thank each of you personally, but I think you'd rather I get back to *Cease*.

Thank you all. If I've forgotten someone, I'm terribly sorry. You know I have a shit memory. You can yell at me later.

ABOUT THE AUTHOR

As a child, JC was fascinated by things that went bump in the night. As they say, some things never change. JC is known for her bad-ass anti-heroes who lure unsuspecting readers into their dark stories and refuse to leave them alone—even once their story is finished. JC is a San Francisco Bay Area native, but has also called both Texas and Louisiana home. She just recently ditched her flip flops for winter boots and now resides in Southwestern Illinois. When she's not torturing her characters for fun, JC drops the pen name and goes by Christina.

JC is the author of the Bayonet Scars series—about an outlaw motorcycle club that starts a war with the Italian mafia.

Find JC on the web…
jcemery.com
@jc_emery
FB/jcemeryauthor
GR/jc_emery

47744326R00150

Made in the USA
Middletown, DE
14 June 2019